HARD CORE LAW

ANGI MORGAN

HARLEQUIN INTRIGUE®

There is never a book without my pals Jan, Robin, Jen, Lizbeth and Janie. Lena Diaz, thanks for the brilliant ideas and personal information you shared about raising a child with diabetes. Tim…I love you, man!

ISBN-13: 978-0-373-69921-6

Hard Core Law

Copyright © 2016 by Angela Platt

Printed in U.S.A.

Angi Morgan writes Harlequin Intrigue novels where honor and danger collide with love. Her work is a multiple contest finalist, RWA Golden Heart® Award winner and *Publishers Weekly* bestseller. When not fostering Labradors, she drags her dogs—and husband—around Texas for research road trips so she can write off her camera. See her photos on bit.ly/aPicADay. Somehow, every detour makes it into a book. She loves to hear from fans at angimorgan.com or on Facebook at Angi Morgan Books.

Books by Angi Morgan

Harlequin Intrigue

Texas Rangers: Elite Troop

Bulletproof Badge
Shotgun Justice
Gunslinger
Hard Core Law

West Texas Watchmen

The Sheriff
The Cattleman
The Ranger

Texas Family Reckoning

Navy SEAL Surrender
The Renegade Rancher

Hill Country Holdup
.38 Caliber Cover-Up
Dangerous Memories
Protecting Their Child
The Marine's Last Defense

CAST OF CHARACTERS

Josh Parker—Major in the Texas Rangers, commander of Company F based in Waco. He lost his wife, Gwen, to leukemia and became a single dad of twins. He's been taking advantage of Tracey's willingness to help out with his children's care. But is he ready to change their relationship?

Tracey Cassidy—She went to work for the Parkers during Gwen's illness and became a family friend. She's the only mom the twins have ever known. But is it time for her to move on with her life?

Jackson & Sage Parker—The four-year-old twins of Josh. Tracey takes care of them while Josh is working a case.

Uncle Carl—Tracey's uncle and former guardian says he only wants to protect her. Does he have an ulterior motive? Is that why she severed all ties with her family?

Tenoreno Family—Texas organized crime family. Isabella Tenoreno has been murdered. Her husband, Paul, awaits trial and might be trying to cut a deal. Xander, their son, is running the business.

Agent George Lanning—He's worked several cases like this before and each time he puts the victim first. Can he do it again without losing his job?

Special Agent Tom McCaffrey—The FBI has assigned him to Josh's case. Is he really in Waco to help?

Bryce Johnson—Lieutenant in the Texas Rangers, Company F. Expert on the Tenoreno crime family.

Prologue

"It was great to meet you. Night." The last of the birthday guests waved from their cars.

Tracey Cassidy stood at the front door waving goodbye to another couple she barely knew. Two sets of little arms stretched around her thighs, squeezing with an appropriate four-and-a-half-year-old grunt.

"What are you two doing up? I tucked you in three hours ago."

"Happy birthday," they said in unison.

Jackson and Sage giggled until the sound of a dish breaking in the kitchen jerked them from their merriment. Their faces, so similar but different, held the same surprise and knowledge that their daddy was in super big trouble.

"Daddy's going to get it now." Sage nodded until her auburn curls bounced.

"Hurry." Tracey patted them on the backsides and pointed them in the right direction. "Back upstairs before the Major has to scoop you up there himself.

You know you'll have extra chores if he catches you down here."

The twins took each stair with a giant tiptoeing motion. It would have been hilarious to watch them, but their dad was getting a bit louder and might come looking for her to help.

"Scoot, and there's sprinkles on Friday's ice-cream cone."

Bribery worked. They ran as fast as their short legs could carry them up the carpeted staircase. Tracey was sure their dad heard the bedroom door close. Then again, he was making enough noise to wake the barn cats.

"Tracey!" he finally yelled, seeking help. "Where's the dustpan?"

Hurrying to the back of the house, she found Major Josh Parker holding several pieces of broken glass in one hand and the broom in the other. A juggler holding his act. Yep, that's what he looked like. He was still completely out of his element in the kitchen. Or the laundry. Good thing he had a maid.

"It should have been in the closet with the broom. Here, let me take these." She reached for the pieces of crystal covered in the remnants of spinach artichoke dip.

"I'm good." He raised the mess out of her reach. "Sorry about the bowl. I thought I was actually helping for once. Damn thing slipped right out of my hand."

"Here, just put it in this." She pulled the covered trash can over to the mess and popped the lid open.

"Hell, Tracey, you don't have your shoes on. This thing splintered into a thousand pieces."

Two forbidden words in one conversation? She'd never seen Josh even the little tiniest bit tipsy. But the group had toasted a lot tonight. First her birthday, then an engagement, then to another couple who'd looked at each other like lovebirds. Then to her birthday again.

"Are you a little drunk?" She ignored his warning and crossed the kitchen to look for the dustpan, which was hanging on the wall of the pantry exactly where it should have been. She turned to tell Josh and walked straight into his chest.

"Well, would you look at that." He cocked his head to the side emphasizing his boyish dimple. "If it had been a snake it would have bitten me."

"Bitten a big chunk right out of your shoulder." She tapped him with the corner for emphasis, but he still didn't back up out of the doorway.

Josh leaned his forehead against the wood and exhaled a long "whew" sound. The smell of whiskey was strong. He had definitely drunk a little more than she'd ever witnessed. Maybe a little more than he should have. But he'd also been enjoying the company of his friends. Something long overdue. Most of his free time was spent with the twins.

"We need a cardboard box or something. This stuff—" He brought the glass from his side to his chest. "It'll bust through plastic."

His head dropped to the door frame and he closed his eyes. This time he relinquished the broken glass to her and backed up with some guidance. She helped him to the table, set a cold bottle of water in front of him and went about cleaning the floor.

Technically, it wasn't her job. She was officially off duty because Josh was home. But she couldn't leave him with his head on the kitchen table and glass all over the place. The kids would get up at their normal time, even if it was a Saturday. And the maid service wouldn't stop back around until Tuesday.

"The way you look right now, this mess might still be here after school Monday."

She moved around the edge of the tiled kitchen avoiding as much of the mess as she could. He was right about one thing, glass was everywhere. She retrieved her sandals from the living room next to the couch. She'd kicked them off while watching the men in Josh's company interact with one another.

The wives hadn't meant to exclude her, but she wasn't one of them. She was the hired help. The nanny. She detested that word and told those who needed to know that she was the child care provider. In between a few bits of conversation, she silently celebrated in the corner. Not just her birthday, but also the achievement of receiving her PhD.

I need to tell him.

She pulled her sandals from where they'd crept under the couch and slipped them on her feet.

"They weren't very…approachable tonight, were they." A statement. Josh didn't seem to need an answer.

One hand scrubbed at his face, while the other held a depleted water bottle. "Sorry 'bout this."

"Hey, nothing to be sorry for. The cake was out of this world."

"Vivian ordered it."

"Yeah, I was sorry she couldn't stay." Josh's receptionist had done her best to keep Tracey involved in the conversations. "Would you sit down before you fall down?"

"I'm not drunk. Just real tired. We've been working a lot, you know."

"I do. I've been spending way too many nights here. The neighbors are going to start talking."

"Let 'em." He grinned and let his head drop to the back of the couch cushions. "They can whinny all they want. And moo. Or just howl at the moon. I might even join 'em."

"I think you need a dog to howl."

Josh's closest neighbor was about three miles away. He did have several horses, three barn cats and let Jim-Bob Watts run cattle on their adjoining field. No one was really going to know if she was there all night or not.

No one but them.

They'd become lax about it recently. Whatever case the Texas Rangers were working on had been keeping him at Company F Headquarters in Waco. The case would soon be over—at least their part in it. She'd gathered that info from one or two of those whiskey toasts.

Tracey looked around the room. Plastic cups, paper

plates with icing, napkins, forks. How could ten people make such a mess? A couple of the women had tried to offer their help, but everyone had seemed to leave at the same time.

Of course, the man now asleep on the couch, might have mentioned it was late. And if she worked in his office, she might misinterpret that as an order to get out. Tracey sighed and picked up a trash bag. What did one more late night matter?

Not like she had any reason to rush back to her campus apartment. She dropped two plastic cups into the bag and continued making her way around the room. She might as well clean up a little. It was mostly throwaway stuff and it wasn't fair to make the twins help their dad.

After all, it had been *her* birthday party.

Josh had his hands full just keeping up with the twins. The floor would be horrible by Tuesday if she didn't pass a mop across it. So she cleaned the floors and stored the cake—not to mention put the whiskey bottle above the refrigerator. On the second pass through the living room, she took a throw from the storage ottoman and covered her boss.

It might be triple-digit weather outside, but Josh kept the downstairs like a freezer. She draped the light blanket across him and his hand latched on to hers.

Josh should be ashamed of himself for letting Tracey clean up while he faked sleep. *Should be*. He wasn't drunk. Far from it. He was hyperaware of every one of Tracey's movements.

"Tonight didn't go exactly like I planned."

"Oh shoot. I don't know why you scared me, but I thought you were asleep. It was fun. A total surprise." She placed her hand on top of his, patting it as if she was ready to be let loose. She also didn't have a mean bone in her body. She'd never intentionally hurt his feelings.

But Josh had to hold on. If he let her go, he might not ever get the courage again. "You're lying. You were miserable. I should have invited your friends."

"It was great. Really." She patted his hand again. "I better head out."

"No." He stood, letting her hand go but trapping her shoulders under his grip. He lightened up. "I mean. Can you stay a couple of minutes? I didn't give you your present."

"But you threw the party and everything."

Was it his hopeful imagination that her words were a little breathier when he touched her? Touching was a rare occurrence now that the twins walked themselves up to bed and didn't need to be carried. Not his imagination. Her chest under the sleeveless summer shirt was rising and falling faster.

One wayward strand of dark red hair that she tried so hard to keep in place was curled in the middle of her forehead. Most of the time she shoved it back in with the rest, but he practically had her hands pinned at her sides. This time, he followed through on a simple pleasure. He took the curl between his fingers and gently tucked it away.

Josh allowed the side of his hand to caress the soft skin of Tracey's cheek. His fingertips whispered across her lips and her eyes closed. It was time. Now. A conscious decision. No spur-of-the-moment accident.

He leaned down as he tilted her chin up. Their lips connected and his hands wrapped around her, smashing her body into his. They molded together and all the dormant parts of his soul ignited.

Four years since he'd really held a woman in his arms. The last lips he'd tasted had been a sweet goodbye. It had been a long time since he'd thought about passion.

Tracey's eyes opened when he hesitated for a split second. He didn't see fear or surprise—only passion waiting for him. He kissed her again, not allowing them time to think or reconsider.

Her lips tasted like the coconut-flavored lip balm she recently began using. But her mouth tasted of the butter-flavored icing from her birthday cake. Lips soft and rich. Her body was toned, yet pliant against him.

Yes, he analyzed it all. Every part of her. He wanted to remember just in case he never got another chance.

Intimacy hadn't been his since... Since... He couldn't allow himself to go in that direction. Tracey was in his arms. Tracey's body was responding to his caresses.

Their lips parted. He wanted to race forward, but they needed a beginning first. He'd worked it all out a hundred times in his head. This was logical. Start with a kiss, let her know he wanted more.

"Okay, that was…surprising for a birthday present."

No doubt about it, her voice was shaking with breathlessness.

"Sorry, that wasn't it. I kept the box at the office so the kids couldn't say anything. It's in the truck." He slipped his hands into his jeans pockets to stop them from pointing to one more thing. One step away from her and he wondered if she was breathless or so surprised she didn't know how to react.

"Josh?"

No.

"It'll just take a sec."

Tracey caught up with him and followed him onto the porch. "Maybe I should go home?" She smiled and rubbed his arm like a pal.

"Right." He slipped his thumbs inside his front pockets. He lifted his chin when he realized it was tucked to his chest.

"It's just… Well, you've been drinking and I don't want…" Her voice trailed off the same way it did when she was sharing something negative about the twins' behavior. She didn't want to disappoint him. Ever.

"Got it." He marched to her car and forced himself not to yank the door off the hinges.

"Don't be mad. It's not that I didn't—"

"Tracey. I got it."

And he did. All he knew about Tracey was that she'd been there for him and the kids. Assuming she felt the same when— Dammit, he didn't know anything about her life outside their small world here.

"I'm going to head out." Purse over her shoulder, she waved from the front door of her car. "Night." She waved and gently shut the door behind her.

Change is a mistake. Nah, he'd had this debate with himself for weeks. It was time to move on. He couldn't be afraid of what might or might not happen.

Tracey's tires spun a little in the gravel as she pulled away. He hoped like hell that he hadn't scared her away. From him, maybe. But she wouldn't leave the twins, right? She was the only mother they'd ever had in their lives.

For a while, he'd thought he admired her for that. But this wasn't all about the kids. He needed her to say that she felt something for him. Because four years was long enough.

He was ready to love again.

Chapter One

Nothing. Two weeks since Josh Parker had kissed her, and then avoided her like the plague. Two weeks and she'd barely seen him. Adding insult to injury, he'd even hired a teenager to watch the kids a couple of nights.

Tracey tilted the rearview mirror to get a better view of Jackson and Sage. They were too quiet. Smiling at each other in twin language. It was ice cream Friday and they'd behaved at school, so that had meant sprinkles. And they'd enjoyed every single colored speck.

The intersection was busier than usual. The car in front of her turned and Tracey finally saw the holdup. The hood was up on a small moving van at the stop sign. She was making her way around, pulling to the side, when another car parked next to the van.

"Tracey, we're hungry," Sage said.

"I know, sweetheart. I'm doing my best." She put her Mazda in Reverse trying to turn around in the street. "Can you reach your crackers, Jackson?"

"Yep, yep, yep," he answered like the dinosaur on

the old DVDs he'd been watching. She watched him tug his little backpack between the car seats and snag a cracker, then share a second with Sage.

"Just one, little man. You just had ice cream."

Two men left the moving van and waved at her to back up. She was awfully close to the other van, but she trusted their directions. Right up until she felt her car hit. She hadn't been going fast enough for damage, but the guy seemed to get pretty steamed and stomped toward her door.

Great what a way to begin her weekend.

The men split to either side of her car, where one gave her the signal to roll down her window. She lowered it enough to allow him to hear her, then she unbuckled and leaned to the glove compartment for her insurance card.

"Sorry about that, but your friend—" Tracey looked up and froze.

Now in a ski mask, the man next to her window shouted, pulling on the door handle, tapping on the window with the butt of a handgun before pushing the barrel inside. "Open the door!"

She hit the horn repeatedly and put the car back into gear, willing to smash it to bits in order to get away. But it was wedged in tight. Once she'd backed up, they'd quickly used two vehicles to block her, parking in front and behind, pinning her car between the three.

Would they really shoot her to carjack an old junker of a Mazda?

"You can have the car. If you want money, it'll take

a little while, but I can get that, too. You don't have to do this." She kept careful control of her voice. "Just let me unsnap the twins and take them with me."

"Get out! Now!" A second gunman shouted through the glass at the passenger door.

Where were all the cars now? Why had she lowered the window an inch to answer this man's question? What if they didn't let her get the kids out? Her mind was racing with questions.

They shouted at her, banging on the windows. The twins knew something was wrong and began to cry. Tracey gripped the steering wheel with one hand and blared the horn with the other. Someone had to hear them. Someone would come by and see what was happening.

"Lady, you get out of the car or I'll blow you away through the window." Gunman One pointed the gun at her head.

"You don't want these kids. Their dad's the head of the Texas Rangers in this area."

With a gun stuck in her face, Tracey didn't know how she was speaking—especially with any intelligence. Her hands were locked, determined to stay where they were. That's when she had the horrible feeling it wasn't a random carjacking.

"You're wrong, sweetheart. That's exactly why we want them," Gunman Two said.

"Shut up, Mack!" Gunman One screamed, hitting the top of the car. "You!" he yelled at her again. "Stop blabbing and get your butt out here before I blow your brains all over those kids."

One of the drivers got out of his box truck with a bent pole. Not a pole. It looked like it had a climbing spike on the end.

"No!" She leaned toward the middle, attempting to block what she knew was coming.

The new guy swung, hitting the window, and it shattered into pebble-size glass rocks. The kids screamed louder. She tried to climbing into the backseat. The locks popped open and three doors flew wide.

Gunman One latched on to her ankles and yanked. Her chin bounced against the top of the seat. Jarring pain jolted across her face. Before she could grab anything or brace herself, her body tumbled out of the car. Twisted, her side and shoulder took most of the fall to the street.

She prayed someone would drive by and see what was happening. She looked everywhere for help. Wasn't there anyone who could intervene or call the police? Her small purse was still strapped across her chest, hidden at her hip. Her cell phone was still inside so maybe she could—

Gunman One flipped open a knife and sliced the strap, nicking her neck in the process. "We wouldn't want you to call Daddy too soon. You got that tape, Mack?" He jerked her to her feet, hitting the side of her head with his elbow. "You just had to play the hero."

"Here ya go, Mack." Gunman Two, already in the car, tossed him duct tape.

Gunman One smashed her face into the backseat window, winding the tape around her wrists. Both of the children were screaming her name. They knew something wasn't right. Both were trapped in their car seats, clawing at the straps then stretching their arms toward her.

"It's okay, guys. No one's going to hurt you." She tried to calm them through the glass. "Please don't do this. Jackson has diabetes. He's on a restricted diet and his insulin level has to be closely—"

Gunman One rolled her to her back and shoved her along the metal edge of the Mazda to the trunk.

Oh my God. They knew. She could tell by his reactions. She was right. It wasn't a carjacking. This was a planned kidnapping of Josh Parker's twins. Gunman One knocked her to the ground. The other men cut the seat belts holding the kids, took them from the car in their car seats, grabbing their tiny backpacks at the last minute.

How could men in ski masks be assaulting her in broad daylight and no one else see them?

"Please take me. I won't give you any trouble. I swear I won't. I…I can look after Jackson. Make sure he doesn't go into shock."

Gunman One pulled her hands. "You won't do, sister. It's gotta be somebody he loves."

"Let him have crackers. Okay? He has to eat every three or four hours. Something," she pleaded. "Sage, watch your brother!"

When this had all started, Tracey hadn't paid attention to what the man coming to her window had looked like. An average guy that she couldn't swear was youngish or even in his thirties. They were all decked out in college gear. She searched this man's eyes that were bright and excited behind the green ski mask, memorizing everything about their brown darkness.

The tiny scar woven into his right eyebrow would be his downfall. He raised the butt of the gun in the air. She closed her eyes, anticipating the blow. The impact hurt, stunning her. Vision blurred, she watched them carry the twins, running to the back of the moving van. Her legs collapsed from the pain, and she hit the concrete without warning.

I'm so sorry, Josh.

Chapter Two

*How were you supposed to tell someone you'd allowed
their kids to be kidnapped?* Tracey would have a doc-
torate in nutrition soon, but none of the courses she'd
taken prepared her to face Josh. Or the future.

When someone found Tracey unconscious on the
sidewalk and the paramedics revived her, she'd cried
out his name. She could never articulate why she was
calling to him. Once fully awake and by the time anyone would listen, the twins had been missing for almost an hour. Tracey hadn't been able to explain to
Josh what had happened. The police did that.

"He's going to hate me," she mumbled.

"I don't think he will. I've dealt with a lot of kidnappings. This isn't your fault. Major Parker will realize
that faster than most." Special Agent George Lanning
had answered her with an intelligent response.

The problem was…

"Intelligence has nothing to do with emotional, gut-
wrenching pain. I lost his kids. He'll never trust me
again and I don't blame him."

After she awoke in the hospital, she'd only been allowed to talk with one police officer, her nurse and a doctor. The door had been left open a couple of inches. She'd recognized rangers passing by, even heard them asking about her. But the officer had refused her any visitors. At least until this FBI agent showed up.

Two hours later she was sitting in a car on her way to the Parker home to face Josh for the first time. Where else was she supposed to go? She'd refused to return to her apartment as they'd suggested. "How bad is my face?"

"As in? What context do you mean?"

She flipped down the passenger mirror to see for herself. "Well, I don't think makeup—even if I had any—would help this." She gently touched her cheekbone that felt ten times bigger than it should. "I don't want to look like..."

"Tracey. Four men yanked you from a car and hit you so hard they gave you a concussion. They kidnapped Jackson and Sage. No matter what you think you could have done differently, those men would still have the Parker twins."

She wiped another tear falling down her cheek. Agent Lanning might be correct. But nothing anyone said would ever make her feel okay about what had happened.

Nothing.

The road to the house was lined with extra cars and the yard—where they needed to park—filled with men standing around. The police escort in front of them flipped on the squad car lights with a siren burst to get people out of the way. Tracey covered her ears.

Everything hurt. Her head pounded in spite of the pain medication the doctor had given her. But she was prepared to jump out of the car as soon as it slowed down. First she needed to beg for Josh's forgiveness. And then find out what the authorities had discovered.

"You really took a wallop," he said. "You should probably get some rest as soon as possible."

She had rested at the hospital, where so much had been thrown at her. Part of the argument for her going home was to sleep and meet with a forensic artist as soon as one arrived. She'd refused, telling Agent Lanning it was useless to draw a face hidden with a ski mask. Then they'd finally agreed to take her directly to Josh.

The sea of people parted and the agent parked next to cars nearer to the front porch. She didn't wait for the engine to stop running. She jumped out, needing to explain while she still had the courage.

Moving quickly across the fading grass of the lawn, she slowed as friends stared at her running inside. She completely froze in the entryway, looking for the straight dark hair that should have towered over most of the heads in the living room. But Josh wasn't towering anywhere. She pushed forward and someone grabbed her arm. A ranger waved him off.

Everyone directly involved in Josh's life knew who she was. The ranger who had spotted her was Bryce

Johnson. He put his hand at her back and pushed the crowd of men out of her way.

"You doing okay?" he asked, guiding her through probably every ranger who worked in or near Waco. "Need anything? Maybe some water?"

She nodded. There was already a knot in her throat preventing her from speaking. She'd assumed a lot of people would be here, but why so many? "Why aren't you guys out looking for the twins?"

Everyone turned their attention to a man near the window seat. But she focused on the twins' dad. Josh looked the way he did the day Gwen had died. From day one, neither of Josh or Gwen had felt like employers. They were her friends. She wanted to be there for him again, but didn't know if he'd let her. He glanced at her, and then covered his eyes as though he were afraid to look at her.

The guy in the suit near the window jerked his head to the side and they left. All of them. Except for a woman and Josh, both seated at the opposite end of the breakfast table. They were joined by Agent Lanning, who pulled out a chair and gestured for Tracey to sit.

It was a typical waiting-on-a-ransom-demand scene from a movie. The three professionals looked the parts of FBI agents. The woman sat at something electronic that looked as if it monitored phone calls. Agent Lanning moved to the back door and turned politely to face the window. The other man, who they both seemed to defer to, uncrossed his arms and tapped Josh on the shoulder.

Josh's head was bent, almost protected between his arms resting on the table. He hadn't acknowledged the fact that nearly everyone had left. He hadn't acknowledged anything.

"I don't know what to say. I'm sorry doesn't seem like enough," she began.

Josh's head jerked up along with the rest of him as he stood, tipping the chair backward to the floor. She winced at the noise. She assumed he'd be disappointed and furious and might even scream at her to get out. But feeling it, seeing it, experiencing the paralyzing fear that they might not get the kids back…

"This might sound stupid, but we need to verify that Jackson was wearing his insulin pump," he whispered without a note of anger.

"Yes. I checked it when I picked him up."

"Thank God. I knew you would. You always do."

The woman opened her mouth but the agent at the window raised a finger. She immediately smashed her lips together instead. Josh covered his face with his hands again. What had she expected? That he'd be— *oh, everything's going to be okay, Tracey. Don't worry about it Tracey. We'll find them together, Tracey.*

"Has anyone seen anything? Said anything?" she asked no one in particular.

"Let's step into the bedroom, Miss Cassidy." The agent by the window took a step toward her.

"She stays," Josh ordered, holding up a hand to halt him. "I want to hear everything firsthand. Same for anything you have to say to me. She can hear it, so she stays."

"All right. I'm Special Agent in Charge Leo McCaffrey and this is Agent Kendall Barlow. No, the kidnappers haven't called. There's been no ransom demand." He pointed to the woman at the table and crossed his arms. "Have you remembered anything else that might help?"

"Not really. A van was broken down. Two men came to my car to help me back up. It seems like one purposely let me reverse into the rental van. Then one came to the passenger window and tapped. I thought they needed my insurance or license or something. They looked like college students until they pulled the masks over their faces. I have to admit that I didn't pay any attention to their faces when they were uncovered." Tracey latched her fingers around the edge of the kitchen chair, hoping she wouldn't fall off as the world spun a little on its side.

"You didn't think that was unusual?" the woman asked.

"Not really. Students walk a lot around here. That part of Waco isn't far from downtown."

It was weird what she noticed about Agent McCaffrey. Average height, but nice looking. His short hair had a dent around the middle like Josh's did when he wore his Stetson. Or after an afternoon with his ball cap on. She glanced at his feet. Sure enough, he wore a pair of nice dress boots. And then she remembered the men abducting her had worn work boots.

"Wait. The men who got out of the moving truck. They both wore an older Baylor shirt from about five years ago. And they all wore the same type of work boots. I could almost swear that they were new and the same brand. The man who…who pulled me from the car…" Everyone looked at her, waiting. "He had dark brown eyes and thick eyebrows. Not thick enough to hide a scar across the right one."

"That's good, Miss Cassidy. Anytime something comes to you, just make sure to tell Agent Lanning. Anything special about the others?"

"I wasn't close to the other two. It all happened so fast that I didn't know what to do." She choked on the last word. She hadn't known. Still didn't.

"When you were questioned at the hospital, you had a hard time remembering the small details, but they'll probably come back." The woman spoke again, pushing a pad toward the center of the table. "You should keep a notebook handy."

"I…uh…couldn't get to the hospital," Josh said loudly. He swallowed hard and shook his head, looking a little lost.

Tracey had never seen that look on his face before. "I didn't expect you to."

"It's just… I haven't been there since Gwen…" Josh looked at her asking her to understand without making him say the words. "I guess I had to have been there once with Jackson." He pushed his hand through his short hair. "But I can't remember when for some reason."

"I know. It's okay," she whispered, wanting to reach out and grab his hand. "You needed to be here."

Major Parker was her employer, but she couldn't stand it. Someone needed to help him. To be on his side like no other person would be. This time she shoved back from the table and her chair was the one that hit the floor. She pushed past Agent McCaffrey and covered Josh with her arms. He buried his face against her, wrapping his arms around her waist as if she were the only thing keeping him from falling off a cliff.

Until two weeks ago, they hadn't hugged since Gwen had died. Had rarely touched each other except for an accidental brush when handing the kids to each other. Then there'd been that kiss.

An unexpected kiss after an impromptu surprise birthday party with several of his friends. A kiss that had thrown her into so many loop-de-loops, she'd been dizzy for days. But it must have thrown Josh for a loop he didn't want. He hadn't spoken to her except in passing. Which was the reason she'd accepted the out-of-state position.

She held him, feeling the rapid beating of his heart through the hospital scrubs they'd given her. They had so much to face and right now he needed to be comforted as much as she did.

Someone at the hospital had said she was just the nanny. She didn't feel like *just* the hired help. She'd avoided that particular title and thought it demeaning when Josh's friends referred to her that way. Months when the rent was hard to come by, her friends asked her why she didn't move in to take care of the twins.

At first it had been because she thought it was a temporary job. Eventually Josh would hire a real nanny. Then she'd been certain Josh would eventually date and remarry, so she hadn't wanted to complicate the situation. And this past year it had been because she was falling in love with him.

Now the word *nanny* didn't seem complex enough for their situation. She'd been a part of the twins' lives from infancy. She'd been told to go home and stay there with a protection detail so she could be easily reached if needed. She was *just* the nanny.

Just the person who provided day care—and any other time of the day care when Josh was on a case. But his lost look was the reason she hadn't obeyed the order.

Technically, Tracey knew she *was* just the nanny. Yet, her heart had been ripped from her body—twice. Once for each child.

She held Josh tight until Agent McCaffrey cleared his throat. She sat in the chair next to Josh. Bryce brought the bottle of water he'd offered when she first arrived and dropped back to the living room doorway.

"Is this a vendetta or revenge for one of the men you've put away?" Tracey asked Josh, who finally looked her in the eyes. "I tried to convince them to take me instead. They said it needed to be someone you loved."

Chapter Three

Someone you loved...

Did she know? Josh searched her face, seeing nothing but concern for his kids. It was on the tip of his tongue to tell her they would have gotten it right if she'd been taken.

That sounds ridiculous.

He didn't want her abducted any more than he wanted the twins to be gone. He reached out, touching her swollen cheek.

"They hurt you." Stupid statement. It was obvious, but he didn't know what else to say. "Of course they did. They took you to the hospital."

He noticed what she was wearing, the streak of blood still on her neck, the bandage at her hairline. Hospital scrubs because her clothes had been ruined.

Time to shed the shaking figure of a lost father. Tenoreno had hit his family—the only place he considered himself vulnerable. But he was stronger than this. He needed to show everyone—including himself. Gathering some courage, he straightened his backbone and placed both palms flat on the table to keep himself there.

He knew what McCaffrey was thinking. The agent had repeated his questions about Tracey's possible motives more than once. Agent Kendall Barlow had been ordered to run a thorough background check on "the nanny." If Tracey heard them call her that she'd let them know she was a child care provider and personal nutritionist.

Definitely not the nanny.

The FBI might have doubts about Tracey—he didn't. First and foremost, she had no motive. They might need to rule her out as a suspect. No one in the room had mentioned Tenoreno by name. But Josh knew who was responsible.

Drawing air deep into his lungs, he readied himself to get started. Ready to fight Tenoreno or whoever he'd hired to take his kids.

"The agents need to know how long Jackson's insulin will be okay. Can you give them more details?" All the extra chatter around him died. He took Tracey's hand in his. "I took a guess, but you know a lot more about it than I do. These guys need an accurate estimate. I couldn't think straight earlier."

"It depends." She drew in a deep breath and blew it out, puffing her cheeks. "There are stress factors I can't estimate. A lot will be determined by what they give the twins to eat, of course. The cartridge can last three days, but he might be in trouble for numerous reasons. They could give him the wrong food or the tube might get clogged. The battery should be fine."

"Hear that everybody? My son has forty-eight hours that we can count on. Seventy-two before he slips into a diabetic coma. Why are you still here?" He used his I'm-the-ranger-in-charge voice.

It worked. All the rangers, cops and friends left the house.

"I'm more worried that Sage might try to imitate what I do with the bolus when he eats. She knows not to touch it. But she also knows that when Jackson eats, I calculate how much extra insulin to give him. She's a little mother hen and might try since I'm not there."

"What's a bolus?" George Lanning asked.

"An extra shot of insulin from his pump. You calculate, it injects." The female agent shrugged. "I read and prepare for my cases."

Josh hated diabetes.

Bryce stayed by the kitchen door. He'd driven Josh and wouldn't leave until he had confirmation of orders that the two of them had already discussed. Unofficial orders when no one had been listening. Ranger headquarters had someone on the way to relieve him as Company F commander. Whoever was now in charge would make certain every rule was followed to the letter and that personnel kept their actions impeccable.

"Everyone is working off the assumption that the Tenoreno family is behind this. Right?" he asked McCaffrey, finally stating what everyone thought.

The FBI agents' reactions were about what he expected. No one would confirm. They zipped their lips tight and avoided eye contact. But their actions were all the confirmation he needed.

The Mafia family connection was the reason the FBI had been called as soon as Josh had received the news. He'd rather have his Company in charge, but the conflict of interest was too great.

Bryce stood in the doorway and shook his head, warning him not to push the issue. They'd talked through the short list of pros and cons about confronting anyone called in to handle the kidnapping.

The more they forced the issue, the less likely the FBI would be inclined to share information. It could all blow up in his face. But it was like a big bright red button with a flashing neon sign that said Do Not Push.

The longer the agents avoided answering, the brighter the button blinked, tempting him to hit it.

"The Tenoreno family?"

Tracey was the only one left who didn't know who they were. She needed to know what faced them because she was certain to be used by the Mafia-like family. No one wanted to explain so it was up to him to bring her up to speed.

Two hours and thirty-eight minutes after Tracey was found unconscious on a sidewalk, his phone rang. Brooks & Dunn's "Put a Girl in It" blasted through the kitchen.

"That's my ringtone for Tracey. They're using her phone. It's the kidnappers."

EVERYONE STARED AT the phone. Only one person moved. Agent Barlow pulled a headset onto her ears, clicked or pushed buttons, then pointed to Agent McCaffrey. It really was like being a part of a scripted movie. Tracey could only watch.

"You know what to do, Josh. Try to keep them on the line as long as possible," Agent McCaffrey said.

Tracey cupped her hands over her mouth to stop the words she wanted to scream. They would only antagonize the kidnappers and would probably get her dragged from the room. She needed to hear what those masked men were about to say.

Agent Barlow clicked on Josh's cell.

"This is Parker." Josh's fingers curled into fists.

"You won't hear from us again as long as you're working with the FBI." The line went dead.

"No. Wait!" Josh hammered his hand against the wood tabletop. But his face told her he knew it was no use.

"What just happened? Shouldn't they let us know how to get in touch with them?" Tracey looked around the room, wanting answers. What did this mean? "You do have a plan, right?"

Agent McCaffrey clasped Josh's shoulder, then patted it—while staring into Tracey's eyes. "That's what we expected."

Everyone's stare turned to Agent Barlow, who shook her head. "Nothing. We've been monitoring for Miss Cassidy's phone, they fired it up, made the call and probably pulled the battery again."

"So we're back to square one." Agent Lanning tapped on the window, silently bringing attention to the suits monitoring the outside of the house.

"We have instructions." Josh stared at the only other ranger left in the house—Bryce.

Tracey was confused. It was as if they were speaking in some sort of code. Or maybe they were stating something obvious and the concussion was keeping her from recognizing it. The others shook their heads.

"You don't want to do that, Josh." Agent McCaffrey kept his cool. He clearly didn't want whatever Josh had just silently communicated to Bryce. "This case is going to be difficult—"

"It's not a case. They're my kids." Josh hit his chest with his fist. "Mine."

"You need our resources." Barlow dropped the headphones on the table.

"I *need* you to leave. I've told you that from the beginning." Josh stood. Calmly this time, without tipping the chair to the floor. "I've played along for the past couple of hours hoping it's not what we thought, but it is. These guys aren't going to play games. They either get what they want or they kill—"

"You can't do this," Barlow said.

The agent seemed a little dramatic, but what did Tracey know?

"Yes, I can. It's my right to refuse your help." Josh gestured for Tracey to lead the way to the back staircase.

"Look…" Agent McCaffrey lowered his voice. "We'll admit that the kidnapping involves Tenoreno.

We assume these men are going to ask you to do something illegal. You're better off if we stay."

"I haven't done anything illegal. You need to go." Josh took the Texas Ranger Star he was so proud of and dropped it in the agent's open palm. "Bryce. You know what to do."

Josh caught Tracey under her elbow and led her up the staircase. They went to the kids' bedroom, where he shut the door.

"What is Bryce going to do?"

"First thing is to get my badge back. I shouldn't have given it to McCaffrey. But the agent wanted it for show in case the kidnappers are watching. I'll surrender it to the new Company commander if they ask me to resign, not before. Then he'll get everyone out of the house. Before the FBI arrived, we assumed we knew who was behind the kidnapping. There's really no other motive. It's not like I have a ton of money to pay a ransom."

Tracey winced, but Josh was looking out the window and couldn't have seen. The twins' kidnapping didn't have anything to do with her. The man said it has to be someone he loves. *He meant someone Josh loves. Right?*

"What if..." She hesitated to ask, to broach the subject that this entire incident might be her fault. She cleared her throat. "What are you going to do without the FBI's help?"

"Get things done. Bryce has already arranged for friends in the Waco PD to watch the agents who will be watching us." He quirked a brow at his cleverness, sitting on the footstool between the twin beds.

His wife's parents had chosen that stool to match a rocker Gwen had never gotten to hold her children in. She'd been too weak. It's where Josh refused to sit. The stool was as close as he'd get. The chair was where Tracey had rocked the babies to sleep.

"Have you told Gwen's parents?"

"There's nothing they could do. McCaffrey thinks it's better to wait."

"The FBI will be following us when we leave the house." He stood again, wiping his palms on his jeans. "They'll wait for me to issue an order to my men. I'd be breaking the law since I've been asked to step away from my command. Then they'll swoop back in like vultures and take control of things."

"Will you?"

"What? Leave? Don't worry." He straightened books on the shelf. "When I do, I'll make sure someone's here with you. Bryce will be close. I won't leave you alone."

"No. That's not what I'm talking about. Will you break the law?"

He gawked at her with a blank look of incredulousness. Either surprised that she'd asked, insulting his ranger integrity. Or surprised that she questioned...

"What are you willing to do to save Jackson and Sage?" She tried not to move the rocker. She was serious and needed to know how far he'd go. "For the record, I'm willing to do anything. And I mean anything, including breaking the law."

Did he look a little insulted as he bent and picked up Jackson's pj's from the floor? Well, she didn't care. It was something she needed to hear him say out loud.

"Don't look so surprised. I've heard about the integrity of the Texas Rangers since the first day I met you. How could I not after listening to the countless kitchen table conversations on the subject? Not to mention this past year when three of your company men might have been straddling the integrity fence, but managed to come out squeaky clean heroes."

"You act like having integrity is a bad thing." He clutched the pajamas and moved to the window instead of placing them back in the dresser.

"Not at all." She stood and joined him, wishing she could blink and make this all go away.

All she could do was wrap her palms around his upper arm, offering the comfort of a friend. Even though they'd been raising his children together for four years, she couldn't make the decisions he'd soon be faced with.

"Are you going to tell me about the Tenoreno family? At least more than what I've heard about them in the news? Are you in charge of the case?"

Josh didn't shrug her away. They stood shoulder to shoulder at the pastel curtains sprinkled with baby farm animals. He stared at something in the far distance past the lake. Tracey just stared at him.

"In charge of the case? No. Company F has prepared Paul Tenoreno's transportation route from Huntsville to Austin. I finalized the details this morning. Now that this…the kidnapping, your injuries…" He paused and took a couple of shallow breaths. "Tenoreno's transport to trial has to be what this is all about. Thing is, state authorities are sure to change everything. It's why they brought the FBI onto the case so quickly."

"Is Tenoreno mixed up in the Mafia like the news insinuates?"

"Tenoreno *is* the Mafia in Texas."

A chill scurried up her spine. The words seemed final somehow. As if Josh had accepted something was about to happen and there was no going back. He hadn't answered her question about how far he'd go. But he wouldn't let the Mafia take his kids. He just wouldn't.

"You need to make me a promise, Tracey."

"Anything."

He removed her hands and crossed his arms over his chest, tilting his head to stare at the top of hers because he was frightened to meet her hazel eyes. Frightened of the desperation she might see in his face.

"Hear me out before you give me what for. I made you the guardian of the twins last year."

"Without asking me?"

"Yeah. I was afraid you'd say no." Josh shrugged and lifted the corner of his mouth in a little smile.

It was Tracey's turn to look incredulous. "Seriously?

When have I ever told you that I wouldn't do something for those kids?"

He nodded, agreeing. "I need you to promise that no matter what happens to me…"

"I promise, but nothing's going to happen to you."

Of course, she didn't know that. This afternoon when she'd headed to the day care to pick up the twins, she wouldn't have believed anything could have happened to any of them. It has been an ordinary day. She'd finally made up her mind to talk with Josh about finding a permanent nanny to take her place.

"You asked what I was willing to do. They're my kids, Tracey. I'll do anything for them, including prison time." Josh still had the pj's wrapped in his hand. "Believe me, that's not my intention, but you have to know it's a possibility."

Was he aware that she was willing to join him? She meant what she'd said about doing anything for Jackson and Sage. And if that meant *she* was the one who went to jail—so be it. And if it came down to it, she'd do anything to keep them with their father.

"Just tell me what to do, Josh."

"Nothing. If Tenoreno's people contact you, tell me. You can't be involved in this. It has to be me." He gripped her shoulders and then framed her cheeks. One of his thumbs skated across the bruised area and settled at her temple. "You got that? *I'm* the one who's going to rescue my kids and pay the consequences."

She believed him. She had to. But she couldn't promise to stay out of his way. She might have the answer. What if money could solve their problem? Even if it wouldn't, now wasn't the time to tell him she'd never let him be separated from the twins.

Chapter Four

Josh pulled Tracey to his chest, wrapping his arms around her, keeping someone he cared about safe. He stared at the green pajamas decorated with pictures of yellow trucks—dump trucks, earthmovers, cranes and he didn't know what else. He used to know.

How long had it been since he'd played in the sandbox with the kids? Since he'd been there for dinner and their bath time?

Mixed feelings fired through his brain. He couldn't start down the regret road. He needed to concentrate on the twins' safety. The overpowering urge to protect Tracey wasn't just because she was an unofficial member of the family.

Tenoreno had hired someone to assault her and steal his children. Her cuts and bruises—dammit, he should have been there to protect her. To protect all of them.

"There has to be something we can do to make this go faster." She pressed her face against his chest and cried.

It was the first time to cry since she'd entered the

house today. He fought the urge to join her, but once a day was his limit. If he broke down again, he wouldn't be able to function. Or act like the guy who might know what he was doing.

A knock at the door broke them apart. Tracey went to the corner table and pulled a couple of Kleenex from the box.

"Yeah?" It could only be one of two people on the other side. Bryce or Agent McCaffrey.

"You fill her in yet?" McCaffrey stepped inside, closing the door behind him.

Tracey looked up after politely blowing her nose; a questioning look crinkled her forehead.

"We were just getting there."

"Here's the phone you can use to contact us. We won't be far away."

"But far enough no one's going to notice." Josh took the phone and slid it into his back pocket.

"Anyone following you will see the obvious cars. They'll lose you after a couple of miles, but George and I will be there."

"Josh?" Tracey said his name with all the confusion she should be experiencing. After all, he'd just demanded the FBI and police leave him alone, get out of his house and off the case.

"It's okay, Tracey. All part of the plan. We need the kidnappers to think I'm in this on my own. No help from anyone. Hopefully that'll limit what they ask me to do."

When he left the house he'd have a line of cars following and hoped it didn't look like a convoy. A bad feeling smothered any comfort he had that law enforcement would be close by.

"So everything you just said—"

"Was the truth. Every word." He shot her a look asking her to keep that info to herself.

He knew that stubborn look, the compressed lips, the crossed arms. It would soon be followed by a long exhale after holding her breath. Sometimes he wanted to squeeze the air from her lungs because she held on to it so long. Each time he knew she wasn't just controlling her breathing. She was also controlling her tongue because she disagreed with what he was saying or doing.

Mainly about the kids.

Lately, it had been about how often he worked late or how he had avoided necessary conversations. Like the one congratulating her on finishing her thesis. Yeah, he'd avoided that because it would open the door to her resignation. What they needed to talk about was serious. She'd most likely accepted a position somewhere— other than Waco. If he could, he'd also like to avoid a conversation about what happened two weeks ago when they'd kissed.

This time, he could see that she didn't believe the lines he was spouting to the FBI. He just hoped that Special Agent McCaffrey couldn't read her like a book, too. Then he might suspect Josh had his own agenda.

"I don't think they'll wait very long to make contact after I leave." The agent unbuttoned his jacket and stuck his hands in his pockets. "My belief is that they knew about Jackson's diabetes and believe it will scare you into following their orders faster. If they didn't, they've seen the pump by now and are scared something might happen to him. Either way, I don't think they're really out to hurt the kids."

Agent McCaffrey stood straight—without emotion—in his official suit and tie. Just how official—they'd find out if he kept their deal to let Josh work the case from the inside.

"But you can't be sure of that," Tracey said. "How can anyone predict what will happen."

Tracey was right about part of Josh's inner core. He was a Texas Ranger through and through. He'd try it the legal way. But if that didn't work, they'd see a part of him he rarely drew upon.

"George said you held up at the hospital exceptionally well, Miss Cassidy."

McCaffrey had a complimentary approach, where George looked like a laid-back lanky cowboy leaning on a fence post. Josh had met George several times on cases. He trusted him. George had given his word that McCaffrey would be on board. But Tracey didn't know any of that history. She had no reason to trust any of them.

"Don't I get a phone for you to keep track of my location?" Tracey asked.

"Actually, yes." McCaffrey handed her an identical cheap phone to what they'd given him. "By accepting this, you're allowing us to monitor it."

The man just didn't have the most winning personality. Josh saw the indignation building within Tracey and couldn't stop her.

"Were you really going to wait for my permission? That seems rather silly to ask. Just do it." Her words seemed more like a dare. She was ready to go toe to toe with someone.

"Tracey. That's not the way things are." Standing up for the FBI wasn't his best choice at this precise moment. Tracey looked like she needed to vent.

"Have you ruled me out as a suspect?" she asked.

Why was she holding her breath this time? Did she have something to hide? Josh opened his mouth to reason with her, but McCaffrey waved him off.

"I have a lot of experience with kidnappings, Tracey. I imagine you're familiar with the statistics that most children are abducted by someone in their immediate family or life. My people ran our standard background check on you first thing. We would have been reckless not to." He leaned against the doorjamb not seeming rushed for time or bothered by her hostility. "A reference phone call cleared you."

Tracey stiffened. She drew her arms close across her chest, hugging herself, rubbing her biceps like she was cold. Her hand slipped higher, one finger covering her lips, then her eyes darted toward the window. She was hiding something and McCaffrey had just threatened to expose whatever it was.

"Tracey, what's going on?"

"We're good, Josh." The agent looked at Tracey.

She nodded her head. "I don't know why I said anything. I was never going to keep you from tracking this phone." Tracey sank to the footstool. "I already told you I'd cooperate and do anything for Jackson and Sage."

The special agent in charge crossed the room and patted Tracey's shoulder. He'd done the same thing to Josh earlier, but it didn't seem to ease Tracey. There was nothing insincere in his gesture. But it seemed a more calculated action, as though McCaffrey knew it was effective. Not because it was real comfort.

Josh wanted to throw the agent out of his kids' room and be done with the FBI. "Do you need anything else?" he asked instead.

"I can't help you if you keep me out of the loop, Josh." McCaffrey quirked an eyebrow at Josh's lack of a reaction. "You've got to work with my people to get the children back. We stick with the plan."

"That's all nice and reasonable, but we both know that there's nothing logical about a kidnapping. You can never predict what's going to happen."

"The quicker you pick up that phone and let us know what they want the better."

"The quicker you clear out of here, the faster they'll contact us." Josh's hands were tied. He had to work with the FBI, use their resources, find the kidnappers. Or at least act like he was being cooperative. He sighed in relief when the agent left and softly closed the door behind him.

What the hell was wrong with him?

His twins had been kidnapped. It was natural to want to bash some heads together. But for a split second there, he'd wanted to just do whatever Tenoreno's men wanted and hold his kids again.

Tracey was visibly shaken by whatever McCaffrey's team had uncovered. His background check five years ago when he'd hired her hadn't uncovered it. And in the time that she'd been around his family, she'd never shared it. He had his own five years of character reference. No one else's mattered.

"I don't know what that was about." He jerked his thumb toward the closed door. *Should he ask?* "Right now I don't care."

"I swear I was never… It's just something I keep private. But I can fill you in. I mean, unless it's going to distract you. This shouldn't be about me."

"Will it make a difference to what's going to happen?" Sure, he was curious, but what if she was right and it did distract him? The FBI didn't think it was relevant. He could wait until his family was back where they belonged. "You know, we have more important things to worry about, so save it."

"Okay." Tracey sat straight, ready to get started. "So how is this going to work? Do you think the kidnappers will use my phone to call yours again? Wait!" She popped to her feet. "We don't have your phone. It's downstairs."

Josh blocked her with an outstretched arm. "If it rings, Bryce will let us know. He'll come up here before he leaves and that won't be until everyone else is out of the house."

They stared a second or two at each other. He wanted to know what she was hiding from him. She bit her lip, held her breath, and then couldn't look him in the eyes.

"Tracey, we have to trust each other. If you don't want to go through with this…"

"Of course I want to help. It's my fault they're missing. I don't know how you're being kind to me at all or even staying alone in the same room. I'm not sure I could do it."

"I don't blame you for what's happened. How can I?" He kept a hand on her shoulder. She didn't fight to get away. "I'm beating myself up that I didn't put a security detail on all of you. If anyone's to blame, it's me. Tenoreno has come after three of my men and their families. Why did I think you or the kids weren't vulnerable?"

"We have to stop blaming ourselves," she said softly. "If you have a plan, now might be the time to share it with me."

"It's not so much a plan as backup. What I said before McCaffrey came in, I meant it. But if I can keep the FBI on my side…we're all better off."

A gentle knock stopped the conversation again. "They've cleared out, Major. I've secured all the windows and doors. Here's your phone." Ranger Johnson said through the door.

Josh turned the knob and stuck out his hand.

"Thanks, Bryce. You guys know what to do. My temporary replacement's going to have a tough time. The other men are going to resent that he's there. They're also going to want to help with the kidnapping. You've got to make the men understand that none of you can get involved and that those orders come from me."

"Good luck. And sir—" Bryce shook his hand, clasping his left on top of it "—let's make sure it's just a temporary replacement. You know we're all here when you need us."

"We appreciate that."

"I think this is one time that One Riot, One Ranger shouldn't apply. I'll take care of things." Bryce walked downstairs.

Tracey gently pushed past Josh, nudging herself into the hall. "I can't stay in their room any longer. And I really think I need a drink."

Josh followed her. "But you don't drink. And probably shouldn't, with a concussion."

"Don't you have some Wild Turkey or Jim Beam? Something's on top of the refrigerator, right? It's the perfect time to start."

"Yeah, but you might not want to start with that." How did she know where he kept his only bottle of whiskey?

"Actually, Josh, I went to college. Just because you've never seen me drink doesn't mean it's never happened. A shot of whiskey isn't going to impair my judgment."

She was in the kitchen, pulling a chair over to reach

the high cabinet before he could think twice about helping or stopping. He sort of stared while she pulled two highball glasses reserved for poker night that had been collecting dust awhile. A finger's width—his, not her tiny fingers—was in the glass and she frowned before sliding it toward him across the breakfast bar.

"Drink up. You need it worse than I do."

He stared at it. And at her.

She suddenly didn't look like a college student. He noticed the little laugh lines at the corner of her eyes and how deep a green they were. It took him all this time to realize she was wearing a Waco Fire Department T-shirt under the baggy scrub top. Something he'd never seen her wear before.

She threw the whiskey back and poured herself another. "Am I drinking alone?"

He swirled the liquid, took a whiff. That was enough for him. Clearheaded. Ready to get on the road. That's what he needed more than the sting and momentary warmth the shot would provide.

Tracey threw the second shot back, closing her eyes and letting the glass tip on its side. Her eyes popped open as if she'd been startled. Then they dropped to the phone that was resting next to his hand, vibrating.

Her hand covered the cell.

His hand covered hers.

"Wait. Three rings. It'll allow the FBI time to get their game face on."

Ring three he uncovered her hand and slid through the password, then pushed Speaker.

"Time for round one, Ranger Parker. You get a new phone from a store in Richland Mall. We'll contact you there in half an hour. Bring the woman."

The line disconnected.

"Do they really think that no one is listening to those instructions he just gave us?" Tracey asked.

"We follow everything he says. He'll try to get us clear of everyone. We get the phone, but the next time he makes contact—before we do anything else—we get proof of life." Josh dropped the phone in his shirt pocket realizing that the kidnappers had just made Tracey a vital part of their plan. "I hoped they'd leave you out of this. We just need to know both kids are okay before I argue to take you out of the equation."

"Of course." She hurried around the end of the breakfast bar, grabbing the counter as she passed.

"You look a little wobbly. You up for this?"

"You probably should have stopped me from drinking alcohol when I have a head injury and they gave me pain meds." Tracey touched her swollen cheek and the side of her head, then winced.

Josh held up a finger, delaying their departure. He walked around her and pulled an ice pack from the freezer, tossing her an emergency compress. "This should help a little." Then he pulled insulin cartridges from the fridge, stuffing them inside Jackson's travel and emergency supplies bag.

Instead of her cheekbone, Tracey dropped the cold compress on her forehead and slid it over her eyes.

"You're right." She took off to the front door. "You should definitely drive."

Proof of life. That's what they needed. He looked around his home. Different from the madhouse an hour ago. Different because the housekeeper had come by this morning. Different because Gwen was no longer a part of it.

Different because Tracey was.

Chapter Five

Josh wandered through Richland Mall with the fingers of one hand interlocked with Tracey's. With the other he held the new phone securely in its sack. No one had the number so the kidnappers couldn't use it for a conversation. He expected someone to bump into him. Or drop a note. Maybe catch their line of sight, giving them an envelope.

"Hell, I don't know what they plan on doing. The dang thing isn't even charged."

"You've said that a couple of times now," Tracey acknowledged. "My head is absolutely killing me and I'm starting to see two of everything. Can we get a bottle of water?"

"Sure."

He kept his eyes open and wouldn't let go of Tracey as he paid for the water at a candy store. She looked like a hospital volunteer in the navy blue scrub top.

"Josh, you are making my hand hurt as much as my head." She tugged a little at his thumb.

"Sorry. I just can't—"

"I know. You're afraid they'll grab me. I get it. But my hand needs circulation. Come on. Let's park it on that bench."

He looked in every direction for something suspicious or a charging station for the phone. Whatever or whoever was coming for them could be any of the people resting on another bench or walking by.

"Here, I'm done. Drink the rest." She capped the bottle and tried to hand it to him.

"No thanks."

"If I drink it, I'll have to leave your side for a few and head into the restroom all alone. I know you don't want that."

"Then throw it away. No one's telling you to drink it." He watched the young man with the baby stroller until he moved in the opposite direction.

"Lighten up, Mack," a voice said directly behind them. "Don't turn around."

Tracey stiffened next to him, the bottle of water hitting the floor. A clear indication that she recognized the voice. The guy behind him tapped on Josh's shoulder with a phone.

"Pass me the one you just bought."

Josh forced himself not to look at the man. No mirrored surfaces were nearby. The guy even covered the phone before it got close enough to see his face in the black reflection of the screen.

"That's good, Major. You're doing good. Now, I know you're concerned about your kids. You can see them when you play the video in about twenty seconds. Just let me get through this service hallway. Yeah, you've got a choice—let me go or follow and lose any chance of ever seeing your brats." The kidnapper tapped the top of Josh's head. "Count to twenty. Talk to ya soon."

Josh had his hands ready to push up from the bench and tackle the guy to the ground.

"No." Tracey pulled him back to the bench. "You heard him. He means it. We have to stay here and let him walk away. You promised to do whatever it took. Remember? So please just turn the phone on and get their instructions."

He listened to Tracey and stayed put. The phone had been handed to them with gloves. Most likely no prints, so he turned it on. He clicked through the menu, finding the gallery.

There were several pictures of the twins playing in a room—sort of like a day care crowded with toys. The video shattered his already-broken heart. Sage was crying. Jackson was "vroom vrooming" a car across his leg and through the air.

A voice off camera—the same as behind them— told them to say hi to their daddy.

"I want to go home." Sage threw a plush toy toward the person holding the phone. "Is Trace Trace picking us up?"

Tracey covered her mouth, holding her breath again.

"Can you remember what you're supposed to say? You can go home after you tell your daddy," the kidnapper lied.

The twins nodded their heads, tucking their chins to their chests and sticking out their bottom lips. They might be fraternal, but they did almost everything together.

"Daddy, Mack says to go to… I don't remember." Jackson turned to his sister, scratching his head with the truck. "Do you remember?"

"Why can't you tell him?" Sage pouted.

"Come on, it has a giant bull." Another voice piped in.

"We've been there, Jacks. It's got that big bridge, 'member?" Sage poked him.

"Can you come there and pick us up, Daddy?" Jackson cried.

"Maybe Trace Trace can?" Sage's tears ran full stream down her cheeks.

"You have twenty minutes to be waiting in the middle of the bridge. Both of you. No cops," a voice said on top of the twins cries.

The video ended. All Josh wanted was to rush to the Chisholm Trail Bridge and pick them up. But they wouldn't be there. Instructions would be there. The guy who'd dropped the phone off would be watching them to make certain they weren't followed.

"Let's go." He wrapped his hand around Tracey's. It killed him to hear his kids like that.

"Are they going to keep us running from one spot to another? What's the point of that? And why have us buy a new phone only to replace it with this one?"

While they were leaving the mall in a hurry would

be the ideal time for a kidnapper to try to grab one or both of them. He locked their fingers and tugged Tracey closer to his side.

"Before we get to the car…" He lowered his voice and stopped them behind a pillar at the candy store. He leaned in close to her ear, not wanting to be over-heard. "We need to look closely where he touched us. He might have planted a microphone."

He dipped his head and turned around to let Tracey check. She smoothed the cloth of his shirt across his shoulders.

"I don't see anything, Josh." She shook her head and turned for him to do the same.

He pushed his fingers through his short hair. Found nothing. Then ran them through Tracey's short wavy strands and over her tense shoulders.

"If I were them, I'd use this time to plant a listening device. I'd want to know if we were really cooperating or playing along with the Feds."

"Who *are you* playing along with?" She looked and sounded exasperated.

"I'm on team Jackson and Sage. Whoever I have to play along with to get them back home. That's the only thing that's important to me."

"All right. So you think they're planting something in the car?"

"Got to be. Or this phone is already rigged for them to listen. Stand at the back of this store and keep an eye out while I call McCaffrey on his phone." Josh took a last look around the open mall area to see if they were in sight of security cameras or if anyone watched them from the sidelines.

Tracey smothered the kidnapper's phone with the bottom of her shirt. "I hope you know what you're doing."

"So do I." He waited for her to get ten feet away from him then took the FBI-issued phone and dialed the only number logged.

As soon as he was connected he blurted, "They have a new phone listed in my name. Bought it prepaid at a kiosk. No idea what the number is. Handed us another and told us to head to the Brazos Suspension Bridge."

"You can cross that on foot. Right?" McCaffrey was asking someone on his staff. "You know they'll be waiting on the other side."

Tracey kept watch, walking back and forth along the wall. She'd look out the storefront window, then make the horseshoe along the outside walls again to look out the other side.

Josh kept his head and his voice down. "I can't contact you on this again. It'll be in the car."

"We'll have men on the north side of the bridge waiting," McCaffrey stated. "Trust me, Josh."

"For as long as possible." He pocketed the phone, waved to Tracey.

"Josh, the kidnapper called you Mack. I remember that they all called each other Mack."

"It kept them from using their real names. Helped hide their identities." He didn't speak his next thought— hoping that they kept their masks on in front of his kids.

They both walked quickly from the mall toward the car.

"We just used five of our twenty minutes. Aren't you going to call Bryce and let him know where we're headed?"

"No need. If the Rangers are doing their job, they'll already know."

Josh pointed to a moving van that matched the description Tracey had regarding the vehicle blocking the intersection. If law enforcement spotted it, they'd be instructed to watch and not detain.

The truck pulled away from the end of the aisle as soon as they reached the car. He was tempted to use the phone, but he'd just proved to himself that they were being watched. He couldn't risk it.

Josh didn't wait around to spot any other vehicles keeping an eye on them. He didn't care if any of them kept up. "Flip down the visor, Tracey." He turned on the flashing lights and let traffic get out of his way. "We're not going to be late."

Tracey braced herself with a foot on the dashboard. "I'm rich. That's my secret."

He slowed for an intersection and looked at her while checking for vehicles. She cleared her throat, waiting. Josh drove. If that was all the FBI could dig up on her, how could that be leverage?

The flashing lights on his car made it easy to get to the bridge and park. He left them on when they got out. Tracey reached under the seat and retrieved a second Jackson emergency kit. He snagged the one he'd brought from the house.

Armed with only a phone and his son's emergency kit, they walked quickly across the bridge to wait in the middle of the river.

"Not many people here on a Friday night." Tracey walked to the steel beams and looked through. "I hope they don't make us jump."

"That could be a possibility." One that he hadn't considered.

"I don't swim well. So just push me over the edge."

"You don't have to go." Josh stayed in the middle, his senses heightened from the awareness of how vulnerable they were in this spot. "How's your head?"

"Spinning. You grabbed extra insulin cartridges and needles. That's what I saw, right? I think I should take a couple, too."

It made sense. He opened the kit. She reached for a cartridge and needle. If the kidnappers took only one of them, they'd each have a way to keep Jackson healthy.

TRACEY WAS SCARED. Out-of-her-mind scared. If today hadn't happened, she would have felt safe standing on a suspension bridge above the Brazos River in the early moonlight with Josh.

But today *had* happened and she was scared for them all.

"What kind of a secret is being rich?" Josh walked a few feet one direction and then back again. "I don't get it. Why is being rich a secret McCaffrey would threaten you with?"

"You really want me to explain right now?"

"You're the one who brought it up." He shrugged, but kept walking. "It'll pass the time."

"My last name isn't Cassidy. I mean, it wasn't. I changed it."

That stopped him. There was a lot of light on the bridge and she could see Josh's confused expression pretty well. He was in jeans and a long-sleeve brick-red shirt that had three buttons at the collar. She'd given it to him on his birthday because she wanted to brighten up his wardrobe. The hat he normally wore was still at home. They'd left without it or it would have been on his head.

"I ran a background check on you. Tracey Cassidy exists."

"It's amazing what you can do when you have money. In fact, I could hire men to help you. My uncle would know the best in the business."

"Let's go back to the part that you aren't who you say you are." The phone in his palm rang. He answered and held it to his ear. "We're here."

Josh looked around the area. His eyes landed on the far side of the bridge, opposite where they'd left the car. Tracey joined him.

"Whatever you want me to do, you don't need my babysitter."

"No, you need me. I can take care of the twins,

change Jackson's cartridge." She held up the emergency pack.

"I don't need any extra motivation. Leave her out of—" He pocketed the phone.

"I'm sorry for getting you into this mess." He hugged her to him before they continued across the bridge then on the river walk under the trees. The sidewalk curved and Josh paused, looking for something.

Another couple passed. Josh tugged on Tracey's arm and got her running across the grass toward the road. If the couple were cops, he didn't acknowledge them. Their shoes hit the sidewalk again and a white van pulled up illegally onto the sidewalk next to Martin Luther King Jr. Boulevard.

The door slid open. That's where they needed to go.

The blackness inside the van seemed final. But she could do this. She'd do whatever it took. Whatever they wanted.

Out of the corner of her eye she saw a man approaching. Then another. The more the two men tried to look as if they weren't heading toward them, the more apparent it was that their paths would. Maybe they were the cops that Bryce had arranged to follow them. If they got any closer, the men inside the van would see them, too.

"What are those guys doing?"

Josh looked in their direction, but yelled at her. "Run. I think they're trying to stop us."

"But—"

"Just run."

It wasn't far. Maybe fifty or sixty feet. The men split apart. Josh dropped her hand. She ran. The van slowly moved forward—away from her. One of the men shot at the van. Then she was grabbed from behind and tripped over a tangle of feet. The man latched on to her waist, keeping her next to him.

"Let me go. I have to get— You don't understand what you're doing."

Another shot was fired. This time from the van. The man's partner fell to the grass. The guy holding her covered her with his body. These men weren't police. The real police raced after the van in an unmarked car, sirens echoing off the buildings across the water.

The man on top of her didn't move and wasn't concerned about his injured partner. She was pounding with her fists on a Kevlar vest trying to get the man off her when a loud crash momentarily replaced the police sirens.

"Oh my God! What have you done?"

Chapter Six

Fire trucks. An ambulance. At least three police cars—maybe more—with strobe lights dancing around in circles. College students edging their way closer in a growing crowd. An angry FBI agent in her face. And a bodyguard who kept insisting that she was too open as she sat on a park bench.

The lights, the voices, the desperation—all made her head swim. Of course it might have been a little remnant of the whiskey. Or possibly the head injury from the kidnappers this afternoon. Maybe both.

Whatever it was, she didn't like it. It was the reason she rarely drank at any point in her life. She simply didn't like being under the influence of anything. Including her uncle Carl, who had taken it upon himself to dispatch bodyguards to protect her. They'd destroyed any chance of getting insulin to Jackson.

The van lay on its side. The driver had escaped before anyone could reach the crash site. Both the guard and Josh had run to the scene, but he was gone. Vanished.

"Miss Cassidy, if you're ready to go. Your uncle instructed us to bring you back to Fort Worth as soon as possible. We've cleared it with the police to pull out." The guard spoke to her with no remorse for what he and his partner had caused. As if she was the most important person in the entire group.

She hated that. She always had.

"How can you stand there and talk as if nothing's happened? Your partner may have shot someone in that van. The driver's disappeared along with the instructions to rescue the twins. What if the kids had been inside? If anything happens to Josh's son—"

"We were just doing our job." He stood in front of her with his hands crossed over each other, no emotion, no whining—and apparently no regrets. His partner had his breath back—which had been knocked out of him by the bullets hitting him in the chest or him hitting the ground.

Jackson and Sage were missing and now the kidnappers would be angry. What would happen now? She needed these men gone. There was only one way to do that. One man. One man could make it happen.

"Let me have your phone."

"Ma'am?"

"I don't have a phone. I need to borrow yours."

He reached inside his jacket pocket, turned on his phone and handed it to her. She searched the call history and found the number she'd almost forgotten. The phone rang and rang some more, going to voice mail, which surprised her. Unless he was with someone—

then nothing would disturb him. Not even the fact that he thought her life was at risk.

Hadn't he sent the guards because he was worried?

A more likely story was that he thought the kidnappers would find out who she was and try to extort money from him. Just the possibility of the family being out any cash would send him into a frenzy to get her safely back inside a gilded cage.

Should she leave a message? She hung up before the beep. What she had to say didn't need to be recorded.

"Where's Josh?" The men standing close to her shrugged in answer. "You do know which man I was with when all this began? The father of the children you just placed in more danger."

The big bulky bodyguard looked like he didn't have a clue. He didn't search the crowd. She followed his gaze to the edge of the people, then across the river where another line of people formed, then back to just behind her where the emergency vehicles were parked.

"Hey. Don't play dumb. I ask. You answer," she instructed, using the power that came with her family name. "And don't think I can't stop your paycheck."

"They moved him to a more secure facility," he finally answered.

"You mean we're trying," Agent McCaffrey corrected as he approached. "I was just coming for you, Tracey. We're heading back to Josh's house. He insists on driving himself but would like to speak with you first."

The agent and bodyguard parted like doors when Josh barreled through them.

"My car's been brought to this side of the river. I'm heading back to my place. You ready?" He extended a hand and she took it.

What would she say to him this time? "Sorry. I should have told you about my powerfully rich uncle who might send bodyguards." Those words didn't roll off her tongue and she'd had no idea he'd send anyone to protect her. Actually, it seemed surreal that he'd found her so quickly.

Josh put his hand on her lower back and guided her through the crowds. Her silent guard followed. The one who hadn't been hit by two bullets in his chest ran toward the road, presumably to get their vehicle.

Josh stopped and did an about-face. "I need to talk with Tracey. Then she's all yours."

"What?" *What did he mean? He was turning her over to her uncle?* She'd been right. Josh wouldn't forgive her this time, but she had something to say about where she went and with whom.

"I can't let her out of my sight, sir." The bodyguard stood more at attention, looking ready to attack. Had he just issued a challenge to a Texas Ranger?

"I don't have time for this. I need to know how you found her." Josh responded by placing his hands on his hips and looping his thumbs through his belt loops. Either to keep from dragging her the rest of the way to his car, or to keep himself from throwing a punch at the bodyguard. She would prefer that he not restrain himself from the latter.

"We tracked her phone. We're assuming it was in the van."

"How did you get the number?" she asked. "I didn't give it to my uncle."

"I have a job to do. And I don't work for either of you."

Josh's hands were pulling the guard's collar together before the man could nod at them both. The guard's hands latched on to Josh's wrists to keep from being choked. Agents who had been watching them closely as they approached the car began running.

If any of them were afraid of what Josh might do, they didn't shout for him to stop. Tracey couldn't bring herself to call out to him, either. After all, it was this man's actions that caused them to lose their main lead to the twins. It was this guy—she didn't even know his name—who had flubbed everything up.

"If you lift one finger…" she said to the guard. But she couldn't blame him or let Josh take out his frustration on the hired help. She'd lost the kids on her watch. She should have been more careful. She laid her hand on Josh's arm, trying to gain his attention. "It's not his fault."

Josh's strong jaw ticked as he ground his teeth. His wide eyes shifted to hers in a crazy gaze, but his muscles relaxed under her fingers.

"Earlier I asked how being rich could be an awful secret." He released the guard shoving him away when two FBI agents were within reaching distance. "I think I have my answer."

"You don't, but I'd rather talk about it in private."

Josh turned and stomped toward his car—the agents close behind.

"Whatever my uncle is paying you, I'll give you the same to stop following me," she said to the bodyguard.

Tracey fell into step next to Agent Barlow, who held up her hand for the guard to stop and not follow. It didn't work. Josh spun around so fast Agent Lanning nearly collided with him.

"No! I need to be alone. That means all of you." He waved everyone away from him. He shook his head, chin hanging to his chest. Then he looked only at her. "They might need you around, but I can't do it. And I don't have to."

"He doesn't mean that," the agent said.

Tracey stopped. Exhausted from everything but really rocked by Josh's words. Her words had been similar when she'd walked away from her uncle when she was twenty-one. She'd left him, the man designated by her parents and grandparents as her guardian, about the same way Josh had disappeared in his car.

Tracey hadn't only meant every word back then, she'd changed her name and began working for the Parkers. Oh yeah, some hurts just couldn't be fixed with "I'm sorry."

Josh drove, heading for the long way home. Flashing lights to warn the cars ahead of him that he was going fast. He was angry. More than angry—he was back to being scared that he'd never see his kids again.

Different than Gwen's last days. That was something he'd prepared for, something he'd known was possible even though he couldn't control it. If those men hadn't shown up, the kidnappers would have given him more instructions. He'd know what he needed to do. Or at least his son would have another insulin cartridge.

There was a blood sugar time bomb ticking away for Jackson, and at the moment Josh had no way to defuse it.

He sped under Lake Shore Drive and realized where his subconscious was taking him—the Rescue Center. He slowed the car to a nonlethal speed and switched off the lights. The phone he'd been given from the kidnappers was still in his back pocket. McCaffrey knew it was there but hadn't obtained the number yet. A true burner that wouldn't lead anyone to his location.

Josh could wait for the kidnapper's next call and instructions. They wanted him to take care of their problem. Right? They had to call back.

Whatever they demanded, he'd do. Alone. No more plans behind the plans or counterespionage. He was on his own and would stay here so no one would find him.

With that decided, Josh parked close to the back door and rang the buzzer. At this time of night there would only be a couple of people on duty. The door opened to a familiar face.

"Hey, Josh. You haven't been around in a while.

What's it been, about six or seven months?" Bernie Dawes stepped to the side, holding the door open and inviting him inside.

Six or seven months ago he'd been thinking about asking Tracey on a date. He'd chickened out. Funny how he could be the tough Texas Ranger ninety percent of the time, making decisions instantly that saved lives. But the possibility of asking a girl on a date caused his brain to malfunction.

"Got any dogs that need to be walked?"

"One of those kinds of nights?" Bernie asked.

"Yeah. I'm waiting on a phone call." Josh stuck his hands in his back pockets, willing the phone to ring. Nothing happened.

"Well, I just took 'em all out about half an hour ago. How about I set you up with an abandoned litter of pups? They've had a pretty rough start."

"That'll do the trick."

Bernie led the way to the kennels and pulled a chair into a small room with a box of four or five black fur bundles. Five. They were all cuddled on top of each other.

"What's on their heads? Are those dots of paint?"

"We've got a Lab that just whelped, so we rotate these dudes in. But they're black, too." Bernie laughed and scooped up one of the pups. "We have a chart with their different colors. It's the only way to tell if they've all been fed. These guys are all full. They just need a little TLC."

"I shouldn't stay long. I might not have much time."

"Whatever you give them is more than they have." He leaned against the wall.

Loving on the puppies was easy. Seeing the other animals—the strays, the injured, the unwanted... The tough guy he appeared to be suddenly needed to know how this man survived day after day. "How do you do this, Bernie?"

He shrugged. "I like animals."

Bernie turned to go, but hesitated. He might have realized that Josh was back because there was a problem. It was like he was the bartender, wiping down the counter a little more often in front of the man sipping his third whiskey.

"I got in trouble today," Bernie said, picking up a puppy. "I didn't mention my wife's hair. She told me to find my own dinner because I didn't notice she had highlights. She's always doing something. I didn't think I had to say anything about it. Sometimes it's the little things that cause you all sorts of big problems. Catch what I'm throwin' at ya?"

Josh nodded. He could still see Tracey as she walked into the kitchen. He'd wanted to look into her eyes and reassure her that everything would be okay, but she'd been staring at the floor. He could only see her thick red hair, messed up as if someone had placed angry hands on her. Seeing her hair like that, he knew she'd been hurt and it killed him.

"Tracey doesn't think I notice that she dyes her hair red." He picked up the first puppy and stroked the entire length of its body. He wasn't completely sure why

Tracey's hair color was important, but he could breathe again. "She started about three years ago, getting a little redder every couple of months. Further away from the brown it used to be."

The room was quiet. No barking or whining. Bernie kept wiping down that metaphorical bar's counter. Josh felt…relief. There weren't too many people Josh could just talk to. He was the commander of the Company. Being a single dad, he didn't go for a drink with the guys after a case very often. It had been a long time since he'd had friends.

"I should have told her I liked it," he admitted.

"Probably," Bernie agreed. "You get that phone call, just make sure the door closes behind you. You come around anytime, man. We understand. Hey, aren't your kiddos old enough to choose a dog? Maybe one of these will do?" He handed the pup with a green dot to Josh. He brushed his hands and gave up waiting on an answer. "Well, I've got a cat who had surgery today and it's having a hard time so I'm going to leave ya to it."

Bernie left in a hurry. Josh figured he must have scowled at the mention of the twins. Poor Bernie thought his visit was about work. Getting a dog? He brought the pup to his face. It was about time. There hadn't been a dog at the house since before he got married.

A whirlwind relationship, elopement and pregnancy that led to Gwen's diagnosis. There hadn't been time to add a dog to the family. Maybe it was part of the reason these types of visits helped. He didn't know who got more out of them—him or the dogs he comforted.

Admit it. The comfort was for him. The idea had come from Company F's receptionist, Vivian. She volunteered for the shelter, trying to place animals and fostering.

The gut-wrenching pain hit him again like it was yesterday. It had been at least a year since he'd felt the loss of his wife so strongly. He put the puppy down and bent forward knowing the pain wasn't physical, but trying to relieve it like a cramp.

When Gwen had been diagnosed with leukemia, every minute of his time had gone to either the job or research or treatment. There had come a time when he'd protected himself so much that he could barely feel.

After the third or fourth late-night trip out here, he'd realized that his unofficial therapy was working. Petting and walking the dogs made him reconnect. He switched puppies and gently stroked, letting the motion replace the fright. It freed his mind. A couple of minutes later he switched again and realized that's why he'd come to the shelter.

It was also a reason he kept the visits to himself. Vivian was the only person in his life that knew he came here to get his head on straight. And he sure needed a minute to think calmly tonight.

The last two pups were smaller than the others. Each had one white paw—one right and one left. He concentrated on those paws and cuddled both of them together. They both almost fit into his palm.

Jackson and Sage had been small. But when they were born they were strong and hadn't needed machines. Trips here to sit with dogs had been fewer when the doctors attacked Gwen's cancer full force. Some days, just taking the time to hold his kids was an effort that made him sleepless with guilt.

The twins were four months old when Gwen realized she was losing the battle. Somehow that had made her stronger. She'd gotten everything in order—with Tracey's help. Gwen fought hard, but in the end, she was at peace that her family would be taken care of.

Removing the phone from his pocket, he replayed the video of his kids. "Ring," he commanded.

He got on his knees next to the box and arranged the blanket where the pups would be secure as they piled on top of each other seeking sleep.

"It can't be over for them. You've got to give me another chance. This can't be the end. She fought so hard to bring these kids into the world," he told the puppies or God or anyone else who might be listening.

The phone rang and he didn't hesitate. "This is Parker."

"You're a very lucky man, Ranger."

"I'm not sure I share your definition of lucky. Does this mean you haven't hurt my kids?"

The insulin cartridges and needles were on the front seat. *Meet me tonight. Ask me to do something right now. I need to make sure my kids are safe.*

"The deal's still moving forward, no matter where you're hiding out."

He heard the uneasiness in the man's voice. Whoever they were, they had no idea that he was at the animal shelter. That might work to his advantage.

"What do you need me to do?"

"You know what we want. Get it. Keep the phone close and wait for instructions."

"Can I talk to Jackson? Is he okay? He has—"

"Diabetes, yeah, we know. We're dealing with it."

"I need to see him, talk to him. His pump and needle will need to be changed. He has to be monitored closely." There wasn't any way he could talk anyone through all the different possibilities that might happen if something went wrong.

"I said we were taking care of it!" the voice yelled. "Don't forget to bring the woman."

"That's not possible."

"Make it possible. Or they'll die."

Chapter Seven

Josh drove to his second home—Company F headquarters. The lights were on and he recognized the vehicles in the parking lot. They were all there. All of his men.

Bryce met him at the door. "We didn't expect to see you, Major. At least not tonight."

"My replacement here?" Josh waited while the ranger secured things, so he could be escorted through the building like a visitor. "I need a minute of his time."

"How you holding up?"

"Can't take time to think about it."

"Captain Oaks is in your office." Bryce led the way through the men.

All of them stood and offered support. They were the best of the best and working the case with or without him as their leader. He entered his office. Nothing had changed. The lifetime he'd been away was actually less than twenty-four hours.

"Aiden." Josh closed the door and dropped the blinds. He didn't want witnesses to the conversation.

Nothing that could hinder the case or put his men at risk of something to testify about later.

Aiden left the chair behind the desk and sat next to Josh. The Captain was much older, but barely looked it. Josh only knew because the "old man," as he was referred to, had been eligible for retirement a couple of years ago. He'd proved his mettle earlier that year when he'd been shot defending the witness of the Isabella Tenoreno murder.

Captain Aiden Oaks had been after the Tenoreno and Rosco Mafia families longer than a decade. It was fitting that he'd take Josh's place as head of Company F.

Even if it was temporary.

"I could ask how you're holding up, but it's obvious. What can I do for you?" Aiden kept his voice low. No chance anyone would overhear them. He also leaned forward, seeming anxious to know what was needed.

There was a chance that Aiden Oaks was the only man in a position of authority who would keep his word. Josh needed to make certain that the captain wasn't going to turn him over to the authorities—state or federal. Or call them as soon as he pulled out of the parking lot.

"They want Tenoreno's transportation route."

"Everyone assumed that's where this was headed." Aiden pressed his lips together into a flat line. "Your men filled me in and headquarters gave me a rough outline before booting me this direction."

"I shouldn't be here." Josh started to rise from the chair, but Aiden coaxed him to sit again. "Just talking to me could get you written up, but I don't have any options."

In his years as a Texas Ranger, Josh had never doubted whether he could count on his partner or the men in his company. If this case was just about him, there'd be no doubt about what he'd do. But his kids' lives had never been dependent on that trust.

Until now.

"I guess the strategy to follow and catch these guys when they weren't looking fell apart when your baby-sitter's bodyguards showed up." Aiden nodded. "Yeah, I'm staying on top of things. But you're here. You obviously have a plan. How can I help put it in action?"

Could he trust this man so intent on helping save his kids?

"I need the route or Jackson dies." Josh watched Aiden's eyes. They never wavered. Never looked away like someone hiding something. "I heard the panic in the kidnapper's voice—both about my son and whatever his original plan was. This character is smart enough to know that he had a short window before everything changed. He's playing it by ear now, just like us."

Aiden nodded again, acting like he understood. "Even if you deliver the route there's no guarantee. Say we give 'em a bit of rope, hoping they might hang themselves, it won't guarantee that your kids will be safely released. Won't mean they'll release you either for that matter."

"But I'll be with them." Josh choked on the words,

took a second, then stood. "My kids aren't going to be the victims in this. I know the limits of the Rangers, of the FBI, of the state prosecutors. They're hoping for an easy fix. We both know there isn't one."

Josh stared at the frame hanging above the door. Gwen stitched the Ranger motto when she'd first been confined to bed rest with the twins. It was a reminder every day of what he'd lost, but he kept it there. Over the last year, it had also become a reminder of what he'd gained—the twins. *And Tracey.*

"One Riot, One Ranger," Aiden said.

Strength and truth were in his voice. Josh had to trust him. His plan could only work if he did.

Aiden gripped his shoulder with a firm, steady hand. "I yanked your company into this mess when I sent Garrison Travis to a dinner party and they witnessed Tenoreno's assassin. I owe you, Josh. So what's the plan?"

Eager to help or eager to learn how to stop him? Aiden might be giving him a long piece of rope to hang himself. It was a risk Josh had to take.

"I need a feasible route, you supply a decoy, we bring these guys down like the rest of the Tenoreno family."

"It's a good start. Are you going to exchange yourself for your kids?"

"That's what I was planning, but I'm not sure it'll work. They're insisting that I bring Tracey."

Aiden rubbed his chin and leaned back in the chair he'd reoccupied. "That does throw a kink in the works.

Could possibly mean that they'll keep all three as hostages until you do whatever they want."

"Yeah, that's the most likely scenario."

"It seems that the only way to get your kids back is to tell the kidnappers the truth. We'll need to inform them how and where Tenoreno is really being moved from Huntsville to Austin. Company F will just have to be prepared."

"Are you going to run this through state headquarters?"

"They won't approve it—not even as a hypothetical." He winked. "Just like they wouldn't have approved the last-minute operation that brought Tenoreno down to begin with. Might be one of those situations where it's better to ask forgiveness than permission. Of course, there's nothing at all to stop us from talking hypothetical situations. Your experience would be valuable and much appreciated."

"My experience. Right." Josh's gut told him to go for it. *Trust him.*

His friend pointed to the motto. "This is one time, more than one of us might be required."

No more stalling. This fight was bigger than just one man. He had to trust that Aiden wouldn't turn him in.

"If I were still in charge of Tenoreno's transport, I'd arrange for air travel. It would be limited ground vulnerability. At this point the state prosecutor is probably scrambling to even make that a private jet."

"I'm not disagreeing with you," Aiden said. "Hypothetically."

In other words, Josh was right. They planned to move Tenoreno from the state prison via plane to Austin for the trial.

"Since we're just talking here, you know what's bothered me? Why did the kidnappers go to so much trouble to put your situation in the public eye? I mean, they could have kept the kidnapping quiet, but they drew you to a popular, normally crowded place."

"If I were Tenoreno's son, a plane is the fastest route out of the country. Huntsville's just a hop into the Gulf and then international waters. All he has to do is hijack the plane."

"That's a fairly sound guess of what they're likely to do." Aiden tapped his fingertips together, thinking.

"Dammit. Is that what all of this is about? Make the kidnapping public so the transfer is by plane instead of car? I thought it was just about gaining access to my credentials so the kidnaper could get close enough to free Tenoreno."

"They manipulated the kidnapping to force you to hijack a plane?" Aiden nodded his head, agreeing, not really asking a question.

"It would make it harder to recapture Tenoreno. Harder for the FBI or Rangers or any law enforcement not to comply since the twins are at risk."

The kidnapping made sense.

"Did you find out why Tracey's uncle sent the guards? Who notified them?"

Josh shook his head, shrugging.

"Too upset? I understand." The older man stood,

joining Josh by sitting on the opposite corner of the desk. "We'll be ready. I guarantee that. And if you just happen to let me see the number you're using on that new phone, then I might have a misdial in my future letting you know what plane and airfield."

Josh turned on the cell and Aiden nodded his head.

"Here's something to ponder while we wait." He jotted down the number. "How did Miss Cassidy's entourage get here? On one hand maybe the kidnappers really want her to take care of the kids. Maybe they just made a mistake not abducting her at the same time. On the other, Xander Tenoreno might have alerted her uncle. That means he knows she's from money. Maybe the kidnappers know too and want a piece of that cash cow."

"How rich is rich?" Josh asked.

"Probably need to have a conversation with the source about that."

Aiden was a wise man. Josh stuck out his hand, grabbing the older man's like a lifeline. It was the first hope he'd had since the van had crashed.

"I can't thank you enough, Aiden."

"I haven't done anything yet. A lot of this depends on you."

Josh looked at Gwen's artwork. "I'll do whatever it takes."

"Just remember, you're not alone."

PULLING A LIGHT throw up to her chin, Tracey curled up as small on the couch as she could get. She closed her eyes, pretending to be asleep, wanting everyone in the house to leave her alone. The FBI agent who'd picked her up at the hospital encouraged her to take the upstairs bedroom.

Josh's room?

George Lanning had no way of knowing she hadn't been in that room since Gwen had gotten very, very ill. It was better to be bothered by people in the living room than to be alone in Josh's bed.

"Miss Cassidy?"

"What?" she answered the bodyguard, who hadn't left her side since coming into her life.

"It's your uncle."

Part of her wanted to tell him to call off these guard dogs and part of her wanted to ignore him—as he'd obviously ignored her for the past several hours. The best thing was to confront the situation and attempt to discover his true motives.

She sat up, tugged her shirt straight and was ready to get to the heart of things. It had been a while since she'd thought of her grandmother's advice when facing a problem. But the words were never truer than at that moment.

Taking the phone, she drew in a deep breath placing the phone next to her ear, ready for an attack.

"Tracey, darling, are you okay?"

"Who is this?" The female voice was a little familiar, but it had been a long time since she'd had contact with her family. She couldn't be sure who it was.

"It's your auntie Vickie, dear. Are you on your way home yet?"

"I don't have an aunt Vickie." At least she hadn't when she'd gone to court to change her name. There hadn't even been a Vickie in her uncle's life. Then again, there'd always been someone *like* a Vickie.

"I know I've met you, dear. I'll admit—only to you—that it's been much too long."

"Where is my uncle? I was told he was calling." She didn't have time to speak with a secretary or even a new wife. She wanted the confrontation over and the guys in the black suits off her elbow.

"Well," the woman's voice squeaked, "he's not really available, but I thought you needed to know that it's important for you to come home."

"Wait, my uncle didn't tell you to call?"

Vickie began a long, in-depth explanation why she'd taken it upon herself to contact her and explain the complexity of the situation in her childhood home. Tracey tuned her out.

Home? The room surrounding her, keeping her warm and safe, was more of a home than any room had ever been in Fort Worth. That place had been more like a museum or mausoleum. Beautiful, but definitely a do-not-touch world.

As a little girl, she'd had the best interior designers. Everything had been pink. She couldn't stand pink for the longest time. Now she had to bite her tongue whenever Sage wanted a dress in the color.

Realizing the phone was in her lap instead of her

hand, she clicked the big red disconnect button and put an end to a stranger's attempt to coax her home. Her new constant companion reached to retrieve it, when it rang again.

Tracey answered herself, more prepared, less surprised. "Yes?"

"Listen to me, you spoiled little brat." Vickie didn't try to disguise the venom. "Carl wants you back here pronto. Niceties aside, you should do what you're told."

"Vickie…dearest—" she could make the honey drip from her voice, too "—I walked away a long time ago. There is absolutely no road for me that leads back there."

The red button loomed. Tracey clicked. It wasn't hard. Not now.

The phone vibrated in her hand. She tossed it to the opposite end of the couch. Totally content with her decision. Her uncle wasn't calling her back and, whoever Vickie was, she couldn't do anything to help save the children.

"I only have two things for you to do," she said to the guard. "My first is that you both get in that car of yours and leave. Without me. The second is not to interrupt me again unless it's really my uncle calling. Period. No secretaries. No Auntie *Vickies* that haven't celebrated as many birthdays as I have. No one except him. And don't say that you don't work for me."

"Yes, ma'am." He nodded and backed up to the door.

What he was acknowledging, she didn't care. Just as long as he stayed next to the door and let her wonder where Josh had gone or whether he was coming back. If she were him she wondered what she'd be thinking.

Before she could lean back into the cushions, the man answered his phone and held it in her direction.

"Speaker, please."

He mumbled into the phone, pressed a button and…

"Tracey? You there?"

She raised her hand, using her fingers to indicate she'd take the call. She popped it off Speaker and paused long enough to fill her lungs again.

"Hi, Uncle Carl."

"You okay, Tracey?" Her uncle didn't sound upset. He might even sound concerned. "I heard there was an accident and a car fire."

"I'm good. My head hurts from earlier, but I'm sure you already have the hospital records."

"It's been a while. I have to apologize for Vickie. She sometimes gets…overly enthusiastic."

"She sounded like it." He hadn't called to talk about his girlfriend, which was the category she could safely put the woman in. He hadn't said anything about getting married. The man was in his fifties and had avoided a matrimonial state his entire life.

"I assume you don't want to come home."

"I am home. My place is here and the men you sent— You did send them, didn't you?"

"As soon as I heard you were assaulted."

"You should have asked me first." As if that step had ever been part of his trickeries.

"You would have said no."

"Of course I would have said no. I work for a Texas Ranger who has a lot of law enforcement access. Why in the world would I need two bodyguards to muck things up?"

"Muck?"

"Yes, Uncle Carl, muck. They arrived and everything became a big mess. Josh is gone, the kids are still in danger, Jackson doesn't have anyone there that understands diabetes. Yes, everything's pretty *mucked* up."

"Mr. Parker's children are in danger?"

"They were kidnapped. That's the reason the FBI called you."

"The FBI? Did they tell you they spoke with me?"

"No. I just assumed that's how you found me." Wasn't that what Agent McCaffrey had insinuated?

"That's ridiculous. I've never *not* known where you are. Just because you changed your name doesn't stop you from being my niece and my responsibility. I'm your guardian, but more importantly, we're family."

It sounded good. The speech wasn't unlike the words that she'd heard most of her life. It did surprise her that he'd known exactly where she was. Well, then again, it didn't. She hadn't gone far.

Same city, same school—she only lived four blocks from the place he'd been paying for. That all made sense. What didn't was his statement that he hadn't heard from the FBI.

"Concern for me was never a problem."

"Ah, yes, you wanted your freedom. Well, anonymously donating to your university down there, did keep me informed."

Same old, same old. Carl was very good at saying a lot of nothing.

"Can we stop this? Just tell me what it's going to take to call off your bodyguard brigade."

"I think you need to sit the rest of this out. Come back here where I can keep an eye on you. Better yet, you've finished your presentation, so why not take a long overdue vacay to someplace breezy. You always liked the beach."

"You're wrong, and this time you have no control over my life." She caught the upward tilt of lips—mostly smirk—of the man at the door. Right. Her uncle's money would always have influence over her life. Money always did. "Just call off your goons."

"That won't be happening. They're there for your safety. You need them." Carl's voice was more than a little smug. As usual, it was full of confidence that his choice was the only choice.

"That couldn't be farther from the truth."

Her uncle never did anything without proper motivation. So what was motivating him this time?

"No need to argue the point any longer, Tracey. I returned your call, answered your questions and have informed you what your option is. Yes, I'm aware you only have one. I must say good night."

"You aren't going to win." It embarrassed her to feel her face contract with a cringe. She knew the words were a fool's hope as soon as she said them.

"My dear, I already have. Those men are not about to leave your side. They'd never work anywhere again. Ever. And they know it."

The phone disconnected and she was no closer to discovering the truth of why her uncle sent the bodyguards. Man, did that sound conceited. Josh would want to know the entire story and specifically that answer when he returned. *If* he returned.

Part of the discussion in the past couple of hours was that Josh had a new phone and it was taking much too long to discover the number. Something to do with finding the kiosk owner, then a person who actually had keys to obtain the sales records. Followed by getting permission to enter the mall.

In other words, they had no clue where Josh was. No one could find him on the road. Some of their conversation had been that the kidnappers may have already contacted him. If so, then at least he had the Jackson emergency kit with him. Josh could monitor his son, save both of his kids.

The bodyguard silently retrieved his phone. He stepped on the other side of the door to take a phone call, but she mostly heard manly grunts of affirmation.

Tracey wanted to run and lock the door. Of course, there wasn't a lock, but it didn't stop her from wanting to be completely alone. She could sulk as good as the rest of them. But it felt ridiculous feeling sorry for herself.

What problem did she have? It was Josh's twins who were missing. Josh would have to do whatever it took to get them back. She could sit here and offer support. Be the loyal day care provider. Her role in the family had been made quite clear when Josh had left her behind.

"Your uncle wants you back in Fort Worth in the morning. We'll leave here at eight sharp, giving you time for some rest." He stood with his back to the door as if he were a guard in front of the Tower of London. Eyes front, not influenced by any stimuli around him.

"I'm not a child and you can't force me to get in a vehicle, especially with the FBI here. I'm not going anywhere. I'm waiting here for Josh." At least she hoped he'd return. "And I'm going to help find his kids. Get with this agenda or leave."

The guard didn't answer. He was a good reflection of her uncle, not listening to her. She curled into the corner of the couch again, pulling the blanket over her shoulder. He was right about one thing—she did need some rest. Because when Josh came back, he would need her help.

And she would be here to give it to him.

Chapter Eight

"Where the hell have you been?" McCaffrey burst through the front door, storming across the porch before Josh had the car in Park.

"Not my problem if your guys can't keep up." He didn't care if the agent thought he was a smart-ass. He had barely been thinking when he'd left the river.

During the twenty-minute car ride from Ranger headquarters, he hadn't come up with a way to get him and Tracey out of the house. It didn't help that he lived in the middle of nowhere and there wouldn't be any sneaking off without guards noticing. Men were everywhere again. One of the bodyguards who had stopped Josh from reaching the van sat in a dark sedan parked in front of the barn.

Bodyguards complicated the equation.

What the hell was he going to do?

"Oh thank God! You're all right," Tracey said when his feet hit the porch. "Can we talk? Let me explain?"

Did he want to go there? Then again, when had it mattered what he *wanted*? Life had proven his wants didn't matter. He had to confront Tracey and talk things out. But when? That was the question he decided was relevant. And who else needed to be confronted—the FBI, local PD or Tracey's bodyguards?

Notably absent was the only organization that held the answer he needed. He had to trust Aiden Oaks, but knew the men in Company F had his back. He'd find out the specifics of moving Tenoreno.

He hadn't been able to speak with Bryce. Maybe find out where their tail had been during the bridge incident and why the rangers had been unable to follow the kidnapper from the van.

If they had, Josh would know. First things first. He had to deal with the people back in his house. McCaffrey was standing on the front sidewalk. Looked like he was first, then Tracey.

"You aren't supposed to be here. Pack it up, Agent."

"Did they make contact with you? Is that the reason you returned?"

"I don't know who's out there watching this conversation. Leave." Josh pointed to the empty dark sedans. Then he turned to the cop on his front lawn. "They have two minutes to clear out or arrest them for trespassing."

"I'm not sure I have that authority," he replied.

"Dammit." Josh glared at McCaffrey. "I probably don't have a choice, but I'm begging you for my kids' lives…leave."

"I have my orders."

Josh was dazed to a point that he couldn't speak.

No words would form. His mind went to a neon sign that flashed. "Jackson might die."

"Josh, come on inside. You can't do this."

Tracey tugged on his hands. Hands that were twisted in the shirt collar circling McCaffrey's neck. How? When? The blackness. It all ran together until everything sort of blurred.

He released the FBI agent and let Tracey lead him inside. He thought she pointed at a man who took care of emptying the room. "How do we get rid of him and his partner?" he asked once he realized it was the second bodyguard.

"Are you okay?"

"Sure. No. I just… I don't know what happened back there." Josh shook his head in disbelief. "I can't remember going for McCaffrey."

"You're upset, exhausted. The stress that you're under is—"

"Things like this don't happen to me. I don't let them." He shrugged away from the comfort Tracey might offer. He wasn't a pacing man.

When he needed to think he lifted his feet up on the corner of his desk and flipped a pencil between his fingers. He paced so Tracey wouldn't be near him. What if he lost it again?

The television in the far corner of the room was muted. No news bulletins. He hadn't expected any since the FBI was keeping a tight lid on things. There hadn't been any Amber Alerts for his kids. Special circumstances, he'd been told.

That part he agreed with. They all knew who had hired the kidnappers. Now they just had to find them.

"I owe you an explanation," Tracey said softly.

"Not sure I can process anything." He scrubbed his face with his palms, desperately attempting to lift the haze. His mind screamed at him not to. If it did, he'd have to find a way to save his kids.

Too late. He was thinking again.

He dropped onto the cushions, breathing fully and under control. For the moment.

"I don't know how to apologize for what happened." She nervously rubbed her palms up and down her thighs. Gone were the scrubs, replaced by regular clothes.

"Forget that for now. Before the van showed up, I asked why being rich needed to be a secret. Have your family problems put my kids in danger?" He shook his head as if he needed to answer that himself and start over. He didn't want to blame Tracey, but the words slipped across his tongue before he could shut himself up. "If I wasn't certain that Tenoreno's people were behind this... Go ahead—explain to me why I should trust you again."

Tracey snapped to attention, cleared her throat, then shrugged. "I was raised like every normal millionaire's kid."

Josh was too tired to be amused until it hit him that Tracey was serious. She sat on the sofa next to him, knee almost touching his leg, hands twisting the corner of a throw pillow, bodyguard at the door.

"You're serious."

"My family's been wealthy for a couple of generations. West Texas oil fields."

"Let me guess. You wanted to see how the other half lived so you went to work as a nanny?"

"I understand why you're mad, but—"

"I'm not sure you do." Josh burst up from the couch with energy he didn't realize he had. *Pace. Get back under control.* "I looked into your bank accounts, Tracey. There wasn't money there. You drive a crappy car. You've lived in the same off-campus apartment for four years. Why? If you have enough money to buy the state of Texas, why are you slumming it?"

"I didn't lie and *I* don't have all the money. My family does. At first, I thought you knew about all this. I told Gwen when she interviewed me who my uncle was. I gave you permission to run a background check. Later, when it was obvious you had no idea about the money, it was nice that you didn't want a favor or something from my uncle."

She thought that he'd want something from her family? Second curve… Gwen had kept this from him. He closed his eyes again. The blackness returned along with the thought he had to get moving. He was ready to move past this, leave and find his children. But he had to understand what he was dealing with regarding the bodyguards and Tracey's family.

"Is Tracey Cassidy your real name?"

"Yes. I legally changed it when I was twenty-one. I

just dropped the Bass. Not that anyone actually associated me with the Bass family in Fort Worth."

He stared at her after she'd thrown two curveballs at him. She was a Bass? As in Bass Hall and the endowments and three of the wealthiest men in Texas?

"Why now? Why have bodyguards come into your life after you've lived in Waco for this long without them? I know they haven't always been hanging around. I think I would have noticed them."

"My parents divorced when I was six. I went to live with my grandparents. They said it was for my own good. Everyone threw the word *stability* around a lot back then. It might have been better. I'll never know. Both my parents remarried, started new families. By then, I was too old and filled with teenage angst."

He paced until he landed in front of the television screen and the dancing bubbles in the commercial. "Were you hiding from your family?"

"No. My uncle controls the trust fund left to me by my grandfather. With that, he thought it gave him complete control of my life. I decided not to let him dictate who was trailing after me in a bulletproof car, or what I did or when. So I left. I walked away from that life."

He couldn't let the bodyguards or Bass family screw things up the next time he received instructions. "Why didn't Gwen tell me about any of this?"

"I honestly thought she had. Look, Josh, my life changed after I walked away from my uncle. I sold my expensive car and lived on the money for almost a year. I had to keep things simple. I had to find a job. I did that through Gwen. She helped before and after I came to work here."

"I wanted her to hire a nurse. In fact, we argued about it a lot." He swallowed hard, pushing the emotion down. "She was right, of course. It was better to have someone she could be... She needed a friend."

"I told her that—the part about a nurse. But she was insistent that you needed a friend, too. She was a very determined woman."

"Yeah, she was."

"I first came here because a secretary in the department wanted to help me make ends meet. I stayed because Gwen asked for my help."

"Why are you still here? I know about the job offer in Minnesota."

She stared at him. Her lips parted, a little huff escaping before she pulled herself straight. Back on the edge of the couch she shook her head as if she couldn't believe what she'd just heard.

"I've spoken to the men who work for my uncle. They said they work for him and he's the only one who can give them new orders." She ignored his question.

The proverbial elephant was sitting in the middle of the room. Neither of them wanted to talk about her leaving. That's why he hadn't discussed the possibility or their accidental kiss.

He had made it a point to work late to avoid talking to her. "I don't have any control of your life, Tracey."

"Of course you don't. I never thought you did."

"You deserve more."

"I seriously don't believe you. After everything we've been through—are going through." She jumped up from the couch. Her sudden movement caught the attention of her guard at the door. He took a look and didn't react. "More of what, Josh? This is *so* not the time to be thinking about my future. We have to get the twins back before Jackson crashes or worse."

"The kidnappers called me."

"What? Why are we talking about me? Do they want money? I can force my uncle—"

"No. It's not about you." He scraped his fingers through his short hair. "It involves you. I mean, I need your help."

"Anything. I already told you."

"I think they want you to come and take care of Jackson. If they'd known about your family, they would have taken you this afternoon."

"I begged them to."

"It's dangerous. This is possibly one of the hardest things I've ever said, but I don't think you should." *Damn!*

"Why would you even think that? You want me to run to safety while Jackson may be...he might be..."

Control. He needed control. But he wasn't going to get it by ignoring that Tracey needed comfort. Or by pretending she wasn't a part of the situation.

She straightened to the beautiful regal posture he'd noticed more than once. "I'll do it. I'm not hiding. I'd never be able to live with myself."

He stood, wanting to go to her. To hold her. Take as

much comfort as he could, possibly more than he was able to offer her.

"If you said that back at the bridge to hurt me…" she sniffed "…maybe to get me back in some way for messing up the exchange at the bridge…well, it worked. I get it. As soon as Sage and Jackson are okay, I'm leaving for Minnesota."

"Yeah." The resignation in his voice was apparent— at least to him. But he hadn't meant it and didn't want her to go. He needed her.

She walked to the window that opened to the back of the house. Sometime in the hour that he was away, she'd gone by her place and picked up clothes. Now she was in jeans, a long-sleeved gold summer sweater over a black lace top.

The boots Gwen had given her for Christmas years ago were on her feet. He recognized the silver toes. She wore them a lot and every time he thought back to that last gift exchange…

So much about her reminded him of his wife. But the strange thing was he'd actually had a longer relationship with Tracey. God, he was confused. Mixed-up didn't sit well. He wasn't a soft or weak guy.

Not being able to concentrate was killing him or would get him killed. What he wouldn't give for the dependability of his men and a solid plan of action. Give him an hour to be in charge and he should be able to resolve this. But he wasn't going to be in charge. He had to accept that.

Thinking like this wasn't helping. Besides, no one

could have predicted that Tracey's uncle would send bodyguards. Or that they'd arrive at exactly that moment.

Whoever was in charge—he stared at the phone still in his possession—a bastard on the other end was dictating the fates of every person he loved.

All he could do was wait.

Tracey sniffed. Her shoulders jerked a little. She was trying to conceal that she was crying. He'd hurt her and been a… Hell, he didn't want to be a jerk.

"I didn't mean it," he said without making a move toward her. "It's just…everything."

"I know. Everything has to work out somehow."

"I need to be doing something."

"Leave."

Josh looked up from his pity party about to ask her where she wanted him to go. But she'd directed her command at the bodyguard still at the slightly open door.

"If you don't leave, I'm going to encourage this… this Texas Ranger to take your head off. Are we clear?" Tracey wrapped her fingers into fists and snapped them to her hips.

With her short hair whipped up like it had just been blown by a big gust of North Texas wind, she almost looked like Peter Pan. Her shapely bottom would never pass for a boy who'd never grown up. But she did look like she was about to do battle.

The bodyguard backed through the door. Tracey took a step forward and slammed it in his face.

"What was that for?"

She spun around and marched across the room. Her battle stance had been switched to face Josh. "No more tears. You think you need action? So do I. What can we do?"

He sputtered a little. The change in her threw him even more off-kilter than he had been. If he'd had any doubts about her, they flew out the window along with the fictional character he'd been envisioning. Tracey was real and very determined.

"When did they contact you?" she asked, hands still on her hips, unwavering.

"How did you—?"

She came in close, taking his hands. "Let's clear the air and get down to business," she whispered. "I understand that whatever might have been developing between us is gone."

Josh wasn't as certain as her upturned face staring at him seemed to be.

"There's only one reason you would have come back here," she continued. "Me."

He deliberately lifted an eyebrow while he glanced at the closed door and searched for the men who'd been passing in front of the windows.

"The only person I've ever worked for is you, Josh Parker. I want to help." She squeezed his hands.

Clarity returned. Her reassurance seemed genuine when he looked into her eyes. As her strength flowed through her grip, sanity returned.

"Whatever it takes. I mean that." The catch in her voice made him want to draw her into his arms again.

Yet, there was something else hanging there, left unsaid. "But?"

She dropped his hands. "We get through this without doubting each other again. But afterward, I'm really leaving. You need to know that."

"I understand." He didn't. Then again, he did.

After knowing her for five years. After trusting her with his children. Yeah, he'd turned on her with a pittance of circumstantial evidence. She was hurt, but there was no going back. He'd lost her trust and maybe even her respect.

Tracey squeezed his left hand—the one where he'd recently removed his wedding ring. Had she noticed? No one in his life had said anything if they had. Another slight tug encouraged him to look at her.

"Now tell me, what do those bastards want us to do?"

Chapter Nine

Tracey had free run of the house. She'd publicly insisted that Josh shower and change, claiming he smelled like dogs. Fingers crossed it made the men watching him less aware of her. She had her fingers on the back door…

"Where are you heading, Miss Cassidy?" Agent Lanning strolled to the breakfast bar, looking as cold as the granite he leaned on.

"I just realized that no one fed the horses yesterday evening." She pointed toward the barn even though it couldn't be seen from the kitchen.

"I'll go with you. It's been a while since I've set foot in a barn." He continued his laid-back attitude and sauntered to the door as if there were no other explanation for her sneaking outside.

He stepped onto the already-dew-soaked grass, paused, lifted the corner of his slacks and tucked them into his boots. "Like I said, it's been a while, but I've done this once or twice."

Great. Just her luck. He really was going to help her. The bottoms of her jeans would be wet by the time they crossed the yard and opened the gate. The agent who'd sat with her at the hospital stretched his arms wide and waved off the bodyguards who would have followed.

The very men she wanted to follow.

"Did Josh leave in the car or his old truck?"

"I beg your pardon?" She tried to look innocent and knew she'd overacted when George Lanning laughed.

"I may not have kids of my own, but I know what I'd do if they were abducted. And that's anything. I've been through this before with my first partner. Josh came back here for a reason. Has to be that the kidnappers decided they need you to take care of Jackson. So is he leaving using the car or the truck?"

She couldn't look directly at him, but saw that his shoulders sort of shrugged. Right that minute, she could see the tall lanky cowboy who seemed to be her friend. But she wasn't easily fooled. Nor was she going to admit she and Josh had planned an escape.

"We've told all of you several times now. That's what the bridge exchange was all about. Or that's what we assumed. And for the record, Josh completely blames me that it got messed up." She tilted her head toward one of her uncle's bodyguards, who followed them across the yard. "I'm not exactly Major Parker's best friend at the moment."

"So it would appear." He waved a gentlemanly hand indicating for her to precede him down the worn path to the barn.

Feeding the horses was a ruse that he'd seen through immediately. She'd had no intention of feeding them at two in the morning, but now she was stuck. At least an extra scoop wouldn't hurt them. And she wouldn't be there when Mark Tuttle came in the morning to clean up and take care of them before school.

George only thought he'd caught her trying to get free. He'd know for certain in a couple of hours—along with everyone else.

They walked through the barn door and right on cue, the bodyguard followed. Josh had come up with several ways for them to leave. That is, once he'd focused and told her what the kidnappers wanted.

Something had changed for the men who had abducted the children. It might have been the fiasco at the bridge, but their fear was that Jackson's condition had worsened. The faster she got to him, the better.

One thing stood in her way—being confined here at the house. She dipped the scoop into the feed, filling the buckets to carry to each stall. Her hand shook so much that some pieces scattered onto the ground.

"You must be pretty scared." George leaned against the post near the first horse, closely watching her actions.

"Any normal, caring human being would be."

"That's right. So I guess you had to explain your background—or should I call it previous life—to Josh." He rubbed his stubbled chin.

"Is my life as a rich girl pertinent to getting the children back?"

"Isn't it?"

"I don't know what you mean."

He nodded toward the bucket. "The horses only missed one meal, right?"

She'd been intently watching his every move instead of paying attention to what she was doing. The bucket now was overflowing onto the floor, making more cleanup for her. The bodyguard snickered a little at her mistake before he clamped his lips together tight and returned to his stoic expression.

"Let me."

George picked up the bucket, held his hand out for the scoop, then finished putting the right amount into each bucket and then each stall. She let him while she wrapped her hand around the handle of a wooden tail brush. This wasn't the original plan, but it was one of its versions.

Josh had argued against it because they didn't know if the bodyguards would fall in line. She had to risk it. When George bent in front of her to scoop up the spilled feed, she raised her hand and let it fall across the back of his head.

She hadn't rendered him unconscious and hadn't expected to. It wasn't a movie, after all. But he did fall face-first into the dirt. She had seconds. "You! Tie him up. We're leaving."

George grabbed the back of his neck and rolled to his shoulder. The man at the door ran quickly forward, for a man of his size. He stuck a knee in the agent's back, practically flattening one of his hands under him.

"Tracey, stop! You don't want to do this," George called.

She looked around for something, anything to stuff

inside his mouth to keep him quiet. The bodyguard yanked George's hands around to his back, looped the lead rope and tied it off. Then he jerked George to a sitting position and tied him to the closest post.

"I don't see anything to keep him quiet."

The guard loosened the tie around George's neck, pulled it up around the man's ears and tightened it enough to quiet any yelling. Then he removed the cell and handgun from under George's jacket.

"Call your partner and tell him to bring the car closer to the gate." She set the cell inside the bucket and stuffed the gun down the back of her pants. That was what everyone always did, right? It didn't seem to want to stay. "Damn." She couldn't run worrying about where the gun would end up and decided to leave it. She grabbed it again and handed it to the guard. "Unload this. Leave the gun, take the magazine."

He followed her instructions. George didn't struggle. In fact, he hadn't put up much of a fight at all. She locked gazes with him and he quirked an eyebrow, then lifted his chin toward the door. "Be careful," was what she could decipher through his muffled speech.

She flipped the barn lights out and waited at the door for her uncle's hired help to make his call. She could see the outline of the car move toward the fence line without its lights. One more look at the agent left behind and she tried not to debate whether George had set her up or helped.

"You know we can take you to a hotel or to your

uncle's, but nowhere else." Her guard placed his hand in the small of her back and gently nudged her forward.

Tracey didn't answer him. They silently moved across the paddock to the far fence. Up and over, then a short distance to where the car waited. Part of her wanted to back out and let him take her to the protection waiting in Fort Worth. Just a small part.

The section of her heart seeking to be fixed needed to find those two kids. It was the half of her that won. She ran to the car and stopped at the driver's door.

"Don't say a word," Josh said, getting out of the car holding a gun on the guard who'd been so helpful. "Your partner's in the trunk. You and I are going to ride in the back. Any trouble, Tracey?"

"George Lanning is tied up in the barn."

Even in the starlight, she could see that Josh was surprised. "Turn around." He cuffed the guard, held the gun until the man got into the car and slid in the back, too.

They didn't need to say anything. She drove to the place off Highway 6 where they'd decided to abandon the guards. It was a long walk back to Waco. She doubted her uncle's men would be picked up by a friendly driver after they'd been forced to strip to their underwear.

"Your clothes will be about a mile down the road." Josh merged onto the road and raised the window.

Less than an hour ago she'd been feeling sorry for herself. "I thought you'd left me behind."

"To be honest, Tracey, I would have. I told you coming back wasn't my choice." Josh shifted in his seat. "I don't want to put you in more danger or ask you to do anything illegal."

"Right. Where to now? They didn't call while I was in the barn. Did they?"

"No."

"So do we need to come up with a plan?"

Josh slowed down on the deserted highway. She dropped the clothes that were in her lap to the edge of the gravel shoulder. The bodyguards would be able to find them easily, and they were far enough off the road not to draw attention.

Josh turned in the seat, facing her.

"Shouldn't we be in a hurry to get away from here?" she asked cautiously.

He tossed the phone they'd bought earlier into the seat between them. "They said they'd call."

"So we wait." She slapped her thighs and rubbed. Nervous tension. She looked around, wondering what he really wanted to say.

The car was still in Drive and his foot was on the brake. No reason to ask if they were going to wait on the guards to catch up with them. Josh kept looking at her and she kept looking everywhere but at him.

"I lied."

"About what?"

"I would have come back. I didn't want to bring you with me to the kidnappers, but I would have come back."

Her mouth was in the shape of an O. She said the

words silently and rubbed her palms against her jeans again. *He would have come back.* Despite everything happening to them, her heart took off a little. She needed hope.

He let off the brake, steered the car onto the road and placed his palm up on the seat covering the phone. It was an invitation, confirmed by the wiggle of his fingers. She accepted, slipping her hand over his and letting it be wrapped within his warmth.

"I think I know what they want me to do, Tracey. There are some good men out there on our side. The ones at the house can't help. George Lanning realized that. I owe him a debt. In fact, I'm going to owe a lot of people when this is over."

"Not me. I'm the one who lost the kids."

He squeezed her hand. "I should have anticipated a move like this from the Tenoreno organization. They've been threatening Company F all year. I never thought... Hell, I just never thought about it. I'm sorry."

"Do you have any place in mind for us to wait? Or are you just driving?" Her stomach growled loud enough to be heard, jerking Josh's stare to her belly. "Have you eaten anything since breakfast?"

"Sounds like you're the one who hasn't." He chuckled. Things were too serious to really laugh. "I don't feel like eating."

"But you need to eat, right?"

"We need to switch cars first." He pulled into a visitor's parking garage at Baylor and followed the signs to park almost on the top floor. Grabbing a bag she hadn't noticed before from the backseat, he pushed the lock and tossed the keys inside before shutting the door.

"You know…it would lower my anxiety level if you'd let me in on whatever plan you've already formed. And don't tell me you don't have one," she finished. He unlocked an older-looking truck. "Aren't you worried about campus security finding the car? Then Agent McCaffrey will be able to figure out what you're driving."

"I'm only worried about Vivian getting in trouble for leaving it. Of course, it'll take them a little while to discover the connection to me. I have high hopes that this is over by then."

"Whose truck is this?" She grabbed an empty fast-food sack and gathered the trash at her feet.

"Vivian's son's best friend. I'm…uh…renting it."

"Not for much, I hope." The half-eaten taco that emerged from under the seat's edge made her gag. "I don't think I'm hungry anymore."

"We should get something anyway. No telling how long it'll be before we can eat again. Looks like we're on empty. Might be good to get Jackson snacks and juice." Josh exited and swung into a convenience store and handed her three twenties without finishing his sentence. "Better pay cash for the gas."

Even with all the media coverage, neither of their pictures had been flashed on the screen—at least from what she'd seen. If she'd had long hair, she would have dropped her head and let it swing in front of her face.

Her hair was the exact opposite. Thick and short and very red, but not very noteworthy.

For Jackson and Sage, she picked up some bottled juice, two very ripe bananas, crackers and animal cookies. Not knowing how much gas Josh was purchasing, she didn't know if she had enough money for a full bottle of honey. She looked in the condiments, but could only pick up grape jelly. That would have to do if—if his blood sugar was too low. She'd have to evaluate him and see.

For them—unfortunately—two overpriced and overcooked hot dogs were in their future. She pointed toward the truck and the teenager behind the counter scanned her items. Josh finished pumping the gas and there was enough cash left for a supersized soft drink for them to share.

The clerk popped her gum and sacked everything. "Want your receipt?"

"No thanks."

Tracey lifted the sack from the counter while the girl continued thumbing through a magazine. It hit her that she'd never experienced that kind of work. Normal young adult work. The only job she'd ever had was helping Gwen and taking care of the kids. It was almost as if she got married her senior year of college, but without all the benefits.

Her life, her classes, her study time were all centered around the Parkers' schedules. That's the reason Josh hadn't known who to invite to her birthday. There wasn't anyone really.

It wasn't his fault. She'd made the choices that had led her to this moment. Josh waved at her to hurry back.

She'd had a very fortunate life. This event didn't seem like it. But they would get the kids back. Josh and the twins would be together again. She took comfort from the way he'd waited to hold her hand. Hopefully that meant there was a place for her in his life, too.

Chapter Ten

"So you have a plan. The Rangers are helping you even though they're not supposed to." Tracey's voice was soft and whispery once the truck engine was off. Josh parked in front of Lake Waco and opened his window.

"The Company isn't involved like you think. I don't have contact with any of them. I won't be sure Aiden is on our side until I get the text with details about the flight. If there is a flight. They might transport Tenoreno some other way."

She rubbed her hands up and down her arms as if she was trying to get warm. Thing was, it had to be ninety degrees outside and he'd cut off the engine quite a while ago. Was she as frightened as he was? Maybe.

He kept his arm across the top of the seat instead of draped over her shoulders where he wanted to put it. Then he extended his hand in an invitation to sit next to him. She took it.

In spite of the trauma and fright, it was a night of firsts. He wanted to hold her because she gave him strength, made him able to face what was coming next.

But he couldn't explain that yet. Not while the kids were missing.

He laced her fingers through hers. The tops of her hands against his palms. His larger hands covered her shaking limbs and she drew them closer around her.

"Want to talk about…anything?" she asked.

"My experience is sort of taking me to the deep end."

"Is that why you're so quiet?"

"I'm quiet?" He never said much. People called him a deep thinker. The Company knew not to interrupt when his feet were up on the corner of his desk. "There's a lot I could tell you. Rain check? It's not the time to think about distractions."

"I look forward to listening and I agree. We need to prepare." She moved their arms as if throwing a punch with each hand.

"Probably. Dammit, Tracey. Do you have any idea how I feel?"

"If your emotions are half as mixed up as mine… Then yes." She squeezed his fingers.

"There's a lot we need to talk about."

"Past, future and present. I know. We've avoided it for quite a while. I understand. I sort of feel disloyal. Then again, I can't help the way I feel."

"You feel disloyal?" he asked, finally looking at Tracey.

"Of course I do, Josh. Gwen was my friend."

He nodded, knowing what she meant. But he also knew that Gwen would want them to be happy…not guilty. When they had the kids back, they'd talk. They'd work it out.

"Do you have any idea what's in store? I know you've worked a couple of missing children cases." She spoke in his direction, but he could only see her in profile.

"Those were more parent abductions. Nothing on this scale."

"But you think they're all right. They wouldn't need me to take care of Jackson if something had happened." She sat straighter, talking to the front windshield. "Wait. You're not sure why they want me, too. Are you?"

"There's a possibility that they've discovered your family has money. They could want that on top of what they want from me. I don't think that's the reason, though."

Tracey relaxed against him, pulling his arms around her like a safety blanket. They shared comfort and intimacy, and the knowledge that they were both scared without having to admit it.

"So everything's just a big mess. I can never tell you how sorry I am about my uncle's interference."

"It wasn't your fault. No need to think about it." In spite of the August heat, she shivered, so Josh hugged her tighter. "I wish there was time to give you some training to protect yourself. It's probably better to get some rest—while you can."

"You think I need self-defense?"

"More like, if you know you're about to be hit—"

He had to clear his throat to say the rest. The thought of her being hit was tearing him apart. "Yeah, if that happens, then turn with the…um…the punch. You'll take less of an impact. But the best-case scenario is to keep your head down and don't talk back."

"In other words, don't give them a reason to hit me. I can do that."

"Right." As much as he loved holding her in his arms, they turned until they could face each other again. "Dammit, Tracey. You can't do this. It's too dangerous. When they call I'm going to tell them you refused."

"No. What if it *is* about the money and not just about Jackson's diabetes? What then? We'll be right back where we are now." She scooted back to the passenger seat. "I totally get why you don't think I can handle this."

"What? That's not it. I have more confidence in your ability to take care of Jackson than I do in mine. It's dangerous, that's all."

"I haven't forgotten how dangerous it is." She rubbed the side of her face that had been hit during the kidnapping.

Josh took her hand in his again. He wasn't going to let tripping over his own words create a misunderstanding. There was a chance that when they faced the kidnappers they may never have another moment—anxious or tender.

"It's not a lack of confidence. I'm just—"

"Shh. Don't say it out loud. It's okay. I am, too."

Afraid. They were both afraid of what was going to

happen to them, to the kids, to their world. Changes were coming.

Dawn was still an hour away as Josh watched Tracey sleep. Her head was balanced on her arm, resting on the door frame, window down with every mosquito at Reynolds Creek Park buzzing its way into the cab.

He swatted them to their deaths in between the cat-naps he caught. He hadn't tried to fall asleep. Maybe if he had, he would have been wide-awake. He'd drifted to the sounds of crickets and lake waves splashing against tree stumps.

The lakeside park was quiet during the early morn-ing. On any usual morning, he would get up, feed the horses, make breakfast, dress the twins and drop them off at their day care before heading into the office. Nor-mal for a single dad.

He wanted to believe that their life was just as nor-mal as the next family's. He heard the whining buzz of another mosquito and fanned the paper sack from the convenience store to create a breeze. The every-day stuff might not be that much different for the kids.

Who could say what normal really was in the twenty-first century? Not him. If he got his family back, who was to say it would ever be normal for them again? Tracey waved her hand next to her ear.

"Ring, dammit."

"What's wrong?" Tracey whispered.

"I'm willing the phone to ring."

"Is it working?" she asked with her mouth in the crook of her elbow.

"Nope."

Normal? Since it was Saturday, he should be waking his kids up three or four hours from now, searching their room for shin guards and taking them to a super peewee soccer game. He should be standing on the sidelines, biting his lip to stop himself from yelling at the twins to stay in their positions and not just chase the ball.

She stretched. "I know how to make it ring. Take me to the restrooms and it's sure to buzz while I'm inside. You know, that whole Murphy's law thing."

"You have a point." He moved the truck up the road and around a corner, keeping the headlights off so as not to wake the campers.

Tracey jumped out. He watched a possum by the park's trash area. It had frozen when the truck had approached. Would his kids be afraid after this? Afraid of strangers? Cars? Afraid of being alone? Were they being kept in the dark? Possibly buried alive?

"Anything?" She'd been gone less than five minutes.

He shook his head and took his turn in the restroom. His movements were slowing and his thoughts progressing at the horrors his kids could be facing right at that moment. The hand dryer finished and he heard Tracey yell his name.

"Should I answer it?" She was out of the truck running toward him.

"Do it."

"Hello?" she said, on Speaker.

"That's good. Glad you could join the party, Tracey."

It was the kidnapper. If his ears hadn't confirmed it, then Tracey's look of fright would have. Her hand shook so much that he took both it and the phone between his.

"Put Jackson and Sage on the phone." He sounded a lot more forceful than he felt. Inside he prayed that they'd both be able to talk to him.

"The brats aren't awake yet and you don't want me to send one of the boys in their room to wake them up."

"I need to know—"

"Nothing! You need nothing. You're going to do whatever I want you to do, whenever I want you to do it."

He was right.

Tracey stared at him, nodded. He couldn't say it was okay. He couldn't admit that this man threatening to harm his children could ask him to do anything…and he would do it.

"What do you want us to do?" she asked.

His heart stopped just like it had the day the doctor told him there was no hope for Gwen. He couldn't move. Tracey's free hand joined his, pulling her closer to the phone. Whose hand was shaking now?

"Wherever you're hiding from the cops, you have fifteen minutes to get to Lovers Leap. Don't be late." *Click.*

"Do you know where Lovers Leap is, Josh?" Tracey shook his arm. "Isn't it over by Cameron Park?"

"Yeah. Sure. I know where it's at."

"Then let's get moving." She tugged on his arm.

"I can't seem to move."

"What's wrong?" Even in the low golden light from the public restroom he could see her concern. She moved to his side, tugged his arm around her shoulders. "Come on. Just lean on me and I'll get you to the truck."

It was slow going, but she managed it. It felt like they used all fifteen minutes of their time, but a glance at his watch told him they still had ten.

"Shock. I think you're in shock and I'm not sure what I can do." She turned the engine over.

"Drive. I'll… I'll be okay when we get there."

He needed to see his kids. Needed to get Tracey there to take care of them. Needed to do whatever these crazy bastards wanted him to, so they'd be free.

Whatever the price. Whatever it took.

"Are you having a heart attack?" She split her focus from the dark road to Josh's pale face.

"I'm okay. Just drive. You have to get to the opposite side of Lake Waco." Josh braced himself in the truck. He rubbed his upper arm, kept it across his chest.

And he was scaring her more than the phone call.

"I think I know where I'm going. You really don't look okay."

"I will be by the time you get there. Quit driving like an old lady."

"Quit trying to change the subject. Do you hurt anywhere? Is your arm numb?"

"I told you I'm not having a heart attack." His voice

was stronger and he pushed his hand against the ceiling as she took a corner a little too sharply. "Whatever it was it's gone. Your driving has scared the life back into my limbs."

Panic attack. Thinking it was okay. Saying it aloud might just make it begin again. She'd never tell. Josh's men didn't need to know that the major of Company F was human.

"Is there any of that soda left? Maybe you need sugar or something?" They were nearing Cameron Park and she had to change her thoughts to what was going to happen. "What if they take me and the kids?"

"Your first priority is the twins. In fact, that's your only priority. Your only responsibility. No matter what they do to me, say about me, or threaten me." Josh shook his head and swallowed hard.

"The same goes for me, Josh. You do whatever it takes to keep Jackson and Sage alive."

"Remember, they seemed a little scared about dealing with Jackson. If you can convince them to drop him off at a hospital, then do it."

"I will." She gave the keys to Josh. He didn't look as pale as when they were at the last parking lot.

"Why did they all call each other Mack? It's confusing."

"Or smart. They call everyone Mack so no real names are used. They wear masks so we can't identify their faces. Hopefully that gives them the security they need not to kill us. So refer to them by body type or what they do. Like the one that gives the orders. He can be In-Charge Mack."

"Is that what you do with the Rangers?" She nervously looked around the park and raced on before he could answer. "No one's here. I wonder if we should get out."

"They're here. There's no vehicle close by. That means they didn't bring the kids. One's on the back side of the restroom building. Another has a rifle behind the north pillar of the pavilion."

The phone was in the seat between them. It buzzed with a text message for her to get out of the car and go with Mack. The second message told Josh to stay.

She tried to brush it off, but admitted, "Josh I'm... I'm scared."

"So am I. I want you to remember this. I'll insist on a video chat when we make contact. They might force you to say whatever they want. I need to know that you and the kids are really okay. So if it's true, then tell me..."

"Something just we know. It'll have to be short."

"Right."

Tracey was nervous. For her, it would be unusual to say I love you. It was on the tip of her tongue to admit that. Thinking like a criminal wasn't her forte, but she understood that they might force her to say those words.

"Let's keep it as simple as possible. Tell me you think you left the whiskey bottle on the counter if you're okay and still in Waco. If you're not okay, play with your ring. If you don't think you're in Waco, then put the whiskey in a friend's house. Can you remember that? Totally off the wall for them, memorable for us."

"What do I say if you can't see me playing with my ring?"

"Say that you wish we hadn't ditched your body-guards." He smiled and took her hand in his and tugged her across the seat. "Come on over here to get out. I can always get back inside if they order me to."

He defied their instructions when his feet hit the ground. Turning to help her from the truck, he pulled her into his arms. Their lips meshed and melted to-gether from the heat of the unknown to come. It was a kiss of desperation, representing all the confusion she'd been feeling for months.

Shoes were hitting pavement behind her. Men were running toward them. She'd already experienced how brutal these men could be.

"You need to be in one piece if you're going to res-cue us," she whispered to the man she was falling in love with. Before any of the kidnappers could grab her she got her hands on Jackson's emergency kit, juice and snacks inside.

Josh cupped her face with his hands. "You're the bravest woman I've ever known. There's no way to thank you." He gently kissed her again.

This kiss felt like goodbye. Sweet, gentle, not rushed in desperation or as fast as her heart that was pound-ing like it would explode.

The men pulled them apart, taking Jackson's bag from her. "Stop. Jackson needs that."

"But you don't. We'll give you what you need when you need it." Tracey fell back a step trying to get out of his way. It was the man who'd hit her. The man who'd been talking to them over the phone…In-Charge Mack.

His cruel eyes peeked through the green ski mask. But they weren't looking at her. No, they watched Josh. They scanned him from head to toe, sizing him up just before shoving him into the side of the truck. Hard.

"When I give an order you better follow it. Don't push me, Major Parker," In-Charge Mack screamed. "Take her to the van."

Birds flew overhead as the world began to brighten. She couldn't see the sun yet, but it was that golden moment where you knew the world was about to be brilliant. She also knew—before his hand raised—that In-Charge Mack intended to hit Josh. It was part of the man's makeup.

The gloved hand moved.

"Stop!" Her hand moved, too. Directly in the path of In-Charge Mack's arm, catching part of the force and slowing him down. "You put me in the hospital. Don't you need Josh without a concussion?"

In-Charge Mack's hand struck as quickly as a snake taking out its prey. The force sent Tracey stumbling into Mack with the rifle. She couldn't see, but she heard the scuffle, the curses, the "don't hurt her" before Josh was restrained by two other men.

"I'm okay. It's okay," she said as quickly as she could force her jaw to move. She looked back at Josh straining at his captors, then at the man who'd hit her. "You need both of us, remember?"

"What I don't need is you talking at all." He gestured with a nod and thrust his chin toward the bike path.

The man who'd grabbed her, slung the rifle over his shoulder and latched on to her arm again. Jerking her toward the park area, she stumbled often from watching Josh instead of the path. When she could no longer see him, she looked in front of her just in time to miss a tree.

The sun was up. Light was forcing the darkness to the shadows. Fairly symbolic for their journey today. She needed good to triumph. She needed hope because they were on their own. Somehow she'd get the twins out of this mire and keep them safe until their dad came home.

THE INSTINCT TO be free was tremendous. The two men holding Josh weren't weaklings by any definition, but he didn't try. He saw the cloth. Then they poured liquid over it. He jerked to the side avoiding their effort to bring him forward.

Chloroform?

Maybe his hunch about the plane wasn't so far off after all. If they felt like they needed him to be out cold for a while, then whatever he was doing wasn't nearby. One of the extras joining the party was digging around the emergency supplies they'd brought. Tracey must have dropped them when she'd been hit.

"Hey! Jackson needs the stuff in that bag."

"Don't worry about your kid. That's why the baby-sitter's here."

"Shut up, Mack," instructed the ringleader. "Put the juice back in the bag and take it to the other Mack."

The guy giving all the orders approached him with the cloth and bottle.

"Look, tell me Jackson's still okay. Is he alert? Talking? How's Sage? Just tell me and I'll behave. No problem. There's no reason to knock me out."

"Your kid is fine."

The guy running the show nodded to the men holding Josh. They planted their feet and tightened their grips. It might be inevitable, but he wouldn't just stand there and inhale peaceably.

Chapter Eleven

Blindfolded. Tracey swore the man driving her to wherever the twins were being held was lost. They had to be close by. It felt like he literally drove in circles. No one had mentioned Jackson or Sage. She thought they'd been joined in the van by a second person back at the park, but the one who'd escorted her could have been mumbling to himself.

You're the bravest woman I've ever known.

A lie. Gwen had been that woman. Strong and fearless in the face of death. But Tracey wasn't going to take Josh's words lightly. She couldn't forget that he'd said them, any more than she could ignore that he was saying goodbye.

The van stopped and so did her thoughts about Josh. Now it was about Jackson. Every piece of knowledge she'd learned and could remember about diabetes would be important.

They'd kept such a close eye on Jackson before yesterday, that he hadn't had any close calls since his initial diagnosis. They even monitored Sage regularly to make certain juvenile diabetes wasn't in her future. There was no guarantee, but they wouldn't be unprepared.

"Get out."

"Can I take off the—"

"Just scoot to the edge and I'll take you inside."

She did what they said. She didn't hear anything unusual. It was still very early in the morning, but there were few natural sounds. She thought she heard the faint—sort of blurry—noise of cars on I-35. The low hum could be heard from multiple spots—and miles throughout Waco. At least she'd be able to find her way to safety.

The twins...your only priority. Your only responsibility.

The men each held one elbow and led her through a series of hallways. She assumed they were hallways. She heard keys in locks, dead bolts turning, doors opening and shutting. Three to be exact.

Inside there wasn't any noise. It was like the world had turned off. Then the blindfold was removed and she blinked in the bright sun reflecting into a mirror. She was still blinking when the fourth door was opened and she was pushed inside. Jackson's emergency bag was tossed in after her.

Thank goodness.

She expected a dark, dingy place. Maybe full of cobwebs or a couple of mice running around. She'd completely forgotten about the video that showed the kids playing with a room full of toys.

They were everywhere. Plastic kitchens complete with pots and pans. Lawn mowers that blew bubbles. A table where they could build a LEGO kingdom on top. Stuffed animals piled in a corner.

Where were the kids?

Who would buy all these toys for a kidnapping? What would be the purpose? She looked closer at them and noticed they were all clean, but very well-used. They were probably from garage sales or thrift shops. Wherever they'd been purchased, no one would remember the person.

But where were the kids?

She picked up one of the many stuffed animals and sat in a chair made for children. Two mostly eaten sandwiches were on the table. Two bottles of water, barely touched, sat next to them. She spotted Sage's backpack under a giant bear. Next to it, her gold glitter slipper.

Tracey crossed the room and bent to pick it up. There, huddled under the pile of used stuffed toys, with their eyes squeezed tightly shut, were the twins. Relief washed over her, but she had to remain calm. Even a little excitement might overtax Jackson's blood sugar at this point.

"Hey kidlets, it's Trace Trace," she whispered, afraid to scare them.

Stuffed giraffes, dinosaurs, bears and alligators flew in all directions as the kids scrambled to their feet. Their backpacks were looped around their shoulders, ready to walk through the door. Shoes on the wrong feet meant they'd been off at least once.

Grape jelly was at the corner of Sage's mouth. But the most important thing was that Jackson looked alert and safe.

"Are you okay?"

She opened her arms and they flew into a hug. The relief she felt that they were both alive and okay... She couldn't think of words to describe the emotion.

"Can we go now, Trace Trace?" Jackson asked. "Where's Daddy?"

"I want to go, too," Sage said. "Why didn't Daddy come get us?"

"Have you had breakfast? Are you really okay?" She turned to Jackson again, gauging his eyes, looking for any indicators that his blood sugar was too low. "Do you have a headache or feel nauseous?"

"Nope."

"He's been good." Sage lifted her hand to her mouth, trying to whisper to Tracey—it didn't work. "I hid the candy they gave us in the oven."

"Oh, I knew where you put it. But I didn't want to get sick if there wasn't anybody here to take care of me."

"Sage, hon, run and get that bag with Jackson's medicine stuff."

The little girl skipped over and skipped back. Both children seemed okay on the outside.

"Do we have to stay?" Sage whined, deservingly so.

"For a little while longer." Tracey pulled the materials she needed to test Jackson's blood sugar from the bag.

The little darling was so used to the routine that he sat with his finger extended, ready for the testing. She put a fresh needle into the lancing device, and took a test strip from the container.

Sage tore the alcohol wipe package open and handed it to her. They all lived with this disease. They'd had their share of ups and downs, but they stayed on top of it.

"I love you guys. Do you know that?" She wiped off the extended finger, punched the button, dropped the droplet of blood on the strip and placed it in the meter.

Two little heads bobbed up and down. She hid her anxiousness waiting on the results. He was in the safe zone, ready to eat his breakfast and start his day.

Thank God.

"Have you two been alone all this time?"

"Nu-uh."

"Some guy sits with a mask all over his face. Says he's hot." Sage was the talker, the observant one, the storyteller. "Then he leaves and comes back sometimes."

"Sometimes he tries to play," Jackson added. "That guy came in with his phone one time. 'Member?"

"Yeah, but he wasn't fun. He was angry and mean."

They sat in the chairs next to her at the table. She put a banana on each little plastic plate. Wiped out the glasses as best as she could and poured a little bit of juice in them. She noticed that one of the juice bottles was missing so she kept a third of the bottle, placing it back in the bag.

"So, eat and I'll get some crackers."

"For breakfast?" they said together.

"There's nothing wrong with bananas and crackers."

"Aren't you eating?" Jackson asked, peeling one section and turning the banana sideways for a bite. He left it there, like a giant smile, then posed until she acknowledged him.

He swallowed his bite and laughed, showing the mashed banana on his tongue. Sage said "yuck," and then they all three laughed, making Tracey want to cry. How could any of this be funny? But if she didn't laugh and act as if it was, then they'd get anxious and stressed.

Stress was bad for blood sugar.

Very bad.

Laughing, playing and maybe casually looking for a way out of this room. That's what their day would be. Maybe the man who was scary and mean would stay away.

Maybe if they were really lucky, Josh would haul all the mean Macks to jail. Then the Parker family could all live happily ever after.

"I want to go home, Trace Trace."

"I know, Jackson. And we will. But while we're here, what do you want to play?"

"Princesses. I thought of something first, so we play my game." Sage darted around looking through the toy pile for princess gear.

"I don't feel like playing." Jackson crawled into her lap and rested his head on her shoulder.

She wasn't going to panic. His level was within normal range. He was outside his routine and would be tired even if he didn't have diabetes. "Okay. Sage, would it be okay if I just told you a story?"

"I can't find any princess hats anyway."

"You know, Sage, you don't have to have a princess hat to be a princess."

"You don't? But isn't it more fun if you do?" She smiled and twirled. "What story are you going to tell?"

"Let's go sit on the mattress so Jackson can take a nap. I mean rest 'cause Prince Jackson doesn't take naps." Then she tickled Sage. "Neither does Princess Sage. Right?"

"Right."

They sat down and Tracey created a story about a prince and a princess who lived with their father, the king. When they asked the king's name she told them King Parker. Sadly, the queen didn't live with them anymore. The story went on and of course the kids recognized that it was about them.

"Then one day a horrible evil dragon swooped down and stole the beautiful princess and handsome prince. The dragon…" The kids held on to her hands tightly and snuggled a little closer. "What should we name the awful dragon?"

"Mack," they said in unison.

"Okay. Mack the dragon was tired of flying around burning up all the bridges. So he went back to the cave where he held the princess and prince. 'What do you want with us?' said the beautiful princess."

Tracey changed voices for each character in the story. The kids were nodding off. Both rested their heads in her lap when one of the Macks came through the door, bolted it behind him and sat on the bench.

She stopped referring to the dragon as Mack. There was no reason to antagonize one of them. And no reason to continue the story since both of the kids were asleep.

Tracey left them curled where they were and propped another blanket behind her head. She pretended to rest and assessed the room through half-closed lids. There didn't seem to be any other way out. The next time they left her alone, she'd be bold and just look.

All those years growing up a rich kid, she'd been warned to be careful. Super careful. She was never allowed to go anywhere alone. Not until her second semester at Baylor.

She remembered the guy who looked like a college student and had followed her around campus. He even had season tickets to football games. Probably not the section he wanted, but her uncle's money had bought him access to a lot.

It took begging her grandfather and whining that she had no friends to get him to call off the hounds. Promising that she'd be overly careful, she was finally on her own. That's when she realized she didn't really know how to make friends.

Then a bad date had shot her overprotective uncle into warlord status. He declared she didn't have any rights and as long as he was paying the bills—blah blah blah. Poor little rich girl, right?

Who would have thought that the first time she'd be placed into real danger would be because she worked for a Texas Ranger? What a laugh her grandfather would have had about this mess.

So there she was, thinking about her grandfather, sitting awkwardly with two precious children asleep on her lap, praying that they'd grow up without being frightened of the world. And then more simply, she just prayed that they'd be able to grow up.

"Trace Trace?" Sage said sleepily. "What happened to the king? Did he get his kids back?" She yawned. "Did he get to be happy?"

"Sure, sweetie. He used his strong sword and killed the dragon. And all the Parkers lived happily ever after."

"Trace…is your name Parker, too?"

"No, kidlet. It's not."

Sage drifted back to sleepy land giving Tracey more time to think about it. She wouldn't be a part of the Parker happy-ever-after. It was time for her to ride into the sunset alone.

Chapter Twelve

Josh lost track of how many times they'd covered his face with the sweet-smelling gauze. Enough for him to have a Texas-size headache. Long enough that his body recognized he'd been in one position too long, lying across the metal flooring of a panel van. And long enough that his stomach thought his neck had been cut off.

The skyline through the van window showed only trees and stars. Definitely not the skyscrapers that would indicate a city. They could still be in Waco, but he had a feeling they'd driven closer to the state prison where Tenoreno was being held.

The men surrounding him were unmasked, but it was too dark to make out any of their faces. Now wearing garb like a strike force—military boots, pants, bulletproof vests, gun holsters strapped to their thighs. Tracey was right. The idea of calling each other Mack tended to be confusing. He had to admit that it was effective. But they didn't act like a cohesive team.

Josh's hands were taped behind him. Tightly. The

hairs on his wrists pulled with each tug he tried to hide. There must be several layers because it wasn't budging. He wouldn't be getting free unless he had a knife.

For the Macks, it had been a good idea to knock him out cold while they traveled. His brain was still fuzzy while he attempted to soak up everything about his situation and process it for a way out. If he'd been awake, the problem would be resolved or at least he'd have a working theory.

Someone kicked the back of his thigh. He held himself in check, but a grunt of pain escaped. He tried not to move. He needed time for the cobwebs to clear. But there wasn't any use trying to hide that he was awake. Even if he wasn't alert.

"Masks on. He's awake."

The thought at the forefront of his mind was Jackson's health and his family's safety. He could only estimate how long his captors had been driving. It might still be early afternoon.

One step at a time.

"I need to talk to Tracey."

If only he could get In-Charge Mack and his men to confirm what they had in store for him. As in why did they need him personally? Whatever it was, they felt like they needed hostages to keep him in line. Once they confirmed, he'd know how to proceed.

Or where to proceed.

"It's time to earn your keep, lawman." The guy who'd kicked him laughed.

They had his phone. Aiden must have texted the location information. Good, they also had his bag from the house. He had a few tricks in there that would help get his family back.

"We're talking to the men that are with her in ten minutes. Behave and you might get an update." The In-Charge Mack didn't even glance back from the front seat.

Laughing Mack looked around, saw where they were, and then pulled a gun to point at Josh's head. "Behave." The gun went under a loose sweatshirt— still aimed at him.

They pulled even with another vehicle, the drivers nodded at each other and separated. He could see the other car lights in the rearview mirror as it did a three-point turn in the road and followed closely behind.

"Where are we?"

"Thanks to you, daddy dearest is scheduled for a private plane ride to get to trial. You're our passport," In-Charge Mack said from up front.

"Daddy? Aren't you a little short to be Xander Tenoreno?"

Laughing Mack kicked out, connecting with Josh's knee.

He'd actually confronted the son of Paul Tenoreno several times. At each encounter he'd looked him straight in the eye. The guy giving the orders here was only about five foot ten. Average height for an above-average criminal.

But he couldn't reject the hunch that these men were regular employees of the Mafia ring in Texas. They were definitely well funded and prepared. The animosity that was associated with their talk about Tenoreno was a bit intense. Why free a man you hated so that he could run the operation again?

"If you'd told me your plans a little earlier, I could have saved you the trouble. They pulled all my authority yesterday when you kidnapped my kids." He wanted to see their reaction. What was their ulterior motive? "I can't get you on that plane."

"Don't be so modest, Major. We have every confidence in your abilities." The one calling the shots turned to show him a picture of Tracey with the kids. "We also have very little confidence that Mack in toy land will keep his cool if you don't get the job done. He's itchy to pull the trigger, don't ya know."

"Isn't it time to stop talking in riddles and tell me what you really want?"

"You haven't figured it out? But you're so good at this. Your Texas Ranger buddies got poor old Mr. Tenoreno moved to the Holliday Transfer Facility. He's waiting to be flown to Austin. We're going to pay him a visit."

"I can't get you inside there, either." Josh attempted to push himself up to a sitting position. His ankles were also taped tightly together. He pushed on a hard-sided case.

"Are you being dense on purpose?" Laughing Mack lashed out with his boot, catching the back of Josh's leg.

"Your kid here is going to make walking anywhere

a problem. Call him off. I need my knees." Josh made note of how many guns were in the van.

"Mack, mind your manners." He spoke to the guy still pointing the gun in Josh's direction, but he pointed twice like he was giving directions to the driver.

Josh used the bumps in the road to help shift his position. He was finally upright and could see more of the view. A field, lots of trees, nothing special out the front. But when he glanced out the back, just behind the second vehicle were soccer and baseball fields.

He knew exactly where they were—Huntsville Municipal Airport. He'd assumed that they'd attack here. He'd just expected a little more time to figure out how to throw a kink in their plan.

"Whatever you're planning, I'm not doing a damn thing until I talk to Tracey. And I mean talk, not just see her picture."

"I figured as much. Almost time."

The van started up, speeding down the dirt road, then pulled under a canopy of trees. The second vehicle pulled in next to them.

"They've left the prison. We have six minutes," the Mack next to him said.

"No Tracey. No cooperation."

"Dial the phone. Remember it's face-to-face and you watch," he told Laughing Mack. "Make it quick."

One thing about this outfit, everyone in it obeyed In-Charge Mack without hesitation. Tracey's face was on the phone screen. She reached out toward the phone at her end, looked sharply away and then back at him.

"They won't let me hold the kids so you can see them but they're doing okay. Sage has been watching over her brother, as usual.'"

"And how is Jackson?"

"He's doing okay. I'm sure he's going to bounce right back after this."

"Have they hurt you?"

"Nothing that a shot of whiskey wouldn't cure. Did I leave it in the middle of the house?"

"What was that?" In-Charge Mack asked.

"She said she wanted some whiskey," Laughing Mack relayed to him.

"That's enough. Disconnect."

"Josh? I wanted to tell you that I—"

Laughing Mack got a big kick out of cutting her off. *Tell me what?*

He didn't have time to process. They opened the van doors and Josh could see the airfield.

"Out."

He lifted his bound ankles and the Mack nearest the door sliced them free with a knife Josh hadn't seen. He really did need to clear his head and become aware of his surroundings. Think this thing through.

The Macks moved the hard-sided case that had been near his feet to outside and flipped the lid open. Machine pistols.

"You really think those are necessary?"

"Glad you asked, Major. Obviously, this is the backup. If you fail, we're bringing down that plane."

"What exactly do you want me to do? I thought you

were here to free Tenoreno." Josh kept his eyes moving. Trying to remember how each of them stood. If they showed any signs of weakness or additional personal weapons.

"Wrong, Major. You're here to kill him."

Chapter Thirteen

Tracey was taking a huge risk. What if they weren't rescued before Jackson needed this cartridge? And what if she *didn't* use the insulin on the sleeping guard? It might be her only opportunity to try to escape. What if Josh didn't—

No! Josh was coming back. He'd never give up and neither would she. She put the kids to sleep on the mattress, leaving their shoes on their feet so they'd be ready. Jackets and bags were by the door. They wouldn't leave without them. It was their routine and no reason to argue.

Taking this risk was necessary, not just a shot in the dark. It would work. She knew what the side effects of too much insulin were. In a healthy person, he'd probably vomit, but he'd eventually pass out. She didn't know how many men were on the other side of the door.

The young man watching them had already complained about how warm it was while wearing the ski mask. The room had its own thermostat. It looked like an old office space. She switched the cool to heat and cranked the temperature up. It was going to be unbearable in a couple of hours. Their guard would get hotter, faster—of course, so would they.

The last thing to do while he was gone from the room was to prep the needle with insulin and hide it. They'd take the emergency kit back and return it to the other room as soon as a Mack came to keep an eye on them. Their ultimate weapon to keep her in line was taking away the emergency kit for Jackson.

"I bet your boss wouldn't like knowing that you don't stay in here while I check Jackson's blood sugar. Nope. None of this would be possible if you did," she said to herself, capping the needle. She couldn't keep it in her pockets. They'd see it for sure.

So she arranged toys and the kid-sized kitchen station near the bench where the guards sat. It was simple to keep the syringe with the toy utensils. She snagged one and put it on the table so she'd have an excuse to exchange it later.

She could give the injection without the guard feeling more than a small prick on his skin. Insulin didn't need a vein, just fatty tissue. If he was sound asleep it might not bother him at all. But she had a sharp toy ready as an explanation. She also moved the trash can closer to the bench…just in case.

They should be coming back into the room soon. She'd been wondering for far too long about life and what the next stage held for her. When all this was done and over, there wouldn't be any waiting. It was so much better to find out. To know.

Leaving Waco, leaving her friends, leaving Josh wasn't her first choice. Waiting wasn't, either. She had to stop being a scaredy cat and start living life. That meant handing in her resignation to Josh and telling him how she really felt.

Forty-eight hours ago she'd been ready to give her notice and walk away. Even if it broke her heart. Well, there was no doubt her heart would shatter now, but it was a resilient organ and she'd manage. She could walk away if Josh didn't ask her to stay.

The locks on the door turned. She dropped her head into her arms on the tiny table and calmed her breathing. She was physically exhausted from a lack of sleep, food and an abundance of adrenaline pumping constantly. Forcing herself to pretend to be asleep might just slow her physical state to let it happen.

Being bent in half like she was wouldn't let her stay asleep for long.

The same guard came straight to the table to collect the emergency kit. She barely saw him through her lashes, watching his silhouette turn off the lamps in the corners, and then sit on the bench.

First step…check.

Rest, rest, rest. She was going to need it to get to safety.

There wasn't a clock in the room and they'd taken her watch—another way to make her dependent on them for Jackson's care. But her body told her she'd been in the cramped position far too long and she hoped her guard was deep in sleep. She pushed her damp hair away from her face.

It was definitely beyond hot.

She took the toy spatula and stood, trying not to make any noise. She'd cleared her path, thinking this through earlier. No squeaky toys, nothing to trip over.

She kept on her toes, not allowing her boot heels to make noise against the linoleum floor. She exchanged the toy gadget for the syringe and removed the needle cover. Still no peep from the kids or their guard. She looked at him; he'd rolled the ski mask up his face, covering his eyes. The smooth chin meant he'd either just shaved or he didn't need to.

The covered eyes meant it would be easier to follow through on her plan. He'd have to move the mask before he could see where she was. She risked a lot by tugging a little at his black T-shirt, but if she could stick this in his side...

Done.

This Mack, sitting on the bench, turned and grunted. He didn't wake. She replaced the cap, threw the syringe away like all the other supplies from earlier and tiptoed to sit on the mattress with the kids.

It didn't take long before their guard moaned, then held his stomach like he was cramping. Before Mack could reach the door, he detoured for the garbage.

Tracey didn't hesitate. She couldn't let herself think about what would happen to the young man. He was a kidnapper. He'd threatened Jackson's life. She was going to make sure the little boy was safe.

No matter the cost. No matter who she had to knock out with insulin to do it. Even in the dim light she could tell he was sweating and disoriented. He was unsteady on his feet and faintly asked for help.

She wanted to. She had to cover her ears, she wanted to help him so badly.

Instead, she got the kids up and sat them in chairs. Jackson was a little woozy and put his head back onto the table. When the young guard began leaning to one side, she struggled with him to put him on the mattress. Then searched his pockets for a cell phone.

Nothing except the keys to the doors.

Before she scooted the twins out of the room, she checked out the other side of the door. No one was there. She ventured farther, listening before she turned each corner. No signs of the other men. She quietly headed back and saw both of their heads poking around the edge.

Backpacks on, they ran to meet her.

"Are we going home now?" Sage asked.

"First we have to play hide-and-seek. You can't giggle or tell anybody where we're at. Okay?"

Both their heads bobbed. Sage jumped up and down, smiled then got Jackson excited as well. "We get to go home. We get to see Daddy." They said in unison, jumping again.

"Please guys, it's really important for us to be quiet. Shh." She placed a finger across her lips and lowered her voice. "Quiet as church mice. Ready?"

They hurried downstairs, where she used the keys again to get out the front door. Austin Avenue?

They were in downtown Waco? It must be the wee hours of the morning, because this was an area of town that was open until two. She hadn't heard any party or loud music. No wonder they'd filled the room with toys to keep the kids occupied and silent.

Tracey ran. She hoisted Jackson to her hip, holding tight to Sage's little hand. "Come on, baby, I know you're tired, but we've got to run. You can do it."

Where to?

They had to be gone—out of view. Fast. Before someone discovered they'd left their room. She tried the sandwich shop next door.

Locked.

They'd all be locked. Everything closed in this part of town. There was nothing to throw at a window. No alarm she could set off without the kidnappers looking out their window and seeing her.

So close.

They were so close to freedom. If they could just find somebody…

Nothing but parking lots, a closed sandwich shop, more parking lots and the ALICO Building. Maybe there was somebody still there.

It was the dead of night and there were no headlights. No one around to wave down for help. They made it across Austin Avenue and then again across Fifth Street. A door banged open. She dared to look back for a split second. It was them.

"Over there," she heard one of the men say.

"Sage, honey, put your arms around my neck." She'd run for their lives carrying the twins. But where?

The parking garage would be open. She ran between the structures. Garage to her left, fire escape to her right. Fire escape? Then what? Climb twenty-two stories outside the tallest building in Waco with twin four-year-olds?

No. All she had to do was make it up one flight before they saw her. The building was split-level—they could hide on the level that was a parking lot. It was more logical to choose the garage door. She couldn't leave their fate to the off chance someone left their car unlocked and they could hide inside.

What then? Blow the horn until their captors broke the window and carried them back to their downtown dungeon?

It would have to be the fire escape. She set a lethargic Jackson on the stair side of the fire escape, helped Sage over and climbed over herself. They were between buildings where the voices of the men chasing them echoed. She didn't know if it could be done, but it was their only chance.

"Quiet as a mouse, kidlets, we've got to keep quiet. Go ahead and start climbing, sweetheart." She adjusted Jackson on her back moving as fast as she could behind Sage.

One foot, then another. Four-year-old legs couldn't take stairs two at a time. Neither could a twenty-six-year-old with a four-year-old on her back. If she wasn't scared of falling down, she would pick up Sage and make the climb with both of them.

The shouts changed. No longer echoes from the street, they were directly below them. Tracey stopped Sage and slowly—soundlessly—pulled her to the side of the building. Maybe they'd get lucky. Maybe neither of the men would look up. Maybe they'd take the logical path into the garage.

Maybe luck was on their side. Looking by barely tilting her head, she watched as the men took off into the other building.

"More quietly than ever, baby girl. We can do this."

It took time. The one flight was actually a little more than that. Their luck ran out. Just as they made it to the roof so did the kidnappers. They yelled out to each other or at someone else, she couldn't be certain.

They were on the lower roof. She set the twins next to a door and looked around for something to pry it open. No junk in the corner. Nothing just lying around to pick up and bang against metal. She heard the men taking the metal fire escape two steps at a time.

Running to the Fifth Street side of the roof, she yelled, "Help! Someone help us!" There weren't any headlights, no one walking, nothing.

Then to the parking lot side toward the river. Someone might be hanging out closer to the water, but it was too far away. "Help! Somebody. Anybody."

Chapter Fourteen

The kids were cuddled together. All Tracey could do was join them. They couldn't tackle the twenty stories of fire escape stairs. Even if they did, there wasn't a helicopter waiting to whisk them off to safety.

The men chasing them heard her cries for help. She heard their shoes slam against the metal steps, then across the roof. She braced herself for punches or kicks. The repercussions of running away. Maybe now. Maybe later. But these men would strike out. She'd protect the kids.

She repeated the promise that they'd be all right as the men both angrily kicked her legs. These men would lose. Josh would find them. They *would* lose.

"Stop it! Don't hurt her!" the twins yelled, still wedged between her and the wall.

Their screams echoed in her ears as they were pulled from her arms. One of the men jerked her up by her hair while the other had a hand on each twin. They struggled. She could barely stand.

He dragged her to the edge of the building, threatening to throw her over the side. His hands went around the back of her neck, pushed her to the ledge. She dropped to her knees.

"I wish I could get rid of you," he spitefully whispered. "I'd leave you on that sidewalk along with the jerk who let you escape. Did you hit him with a stuffed unicorn?" He shoved her forward into the concrete barrier. "Get up and get hold of one of them brats."

Limping down the fire escape, she wondered if they'd care that their friend might die from the insulin injection. She carried Jackson, and poor Sage was in the arms of the man to her right.

The men constantly looked over their shoulders, but they weren't followed. No one drove by. No police were in sight. They weren't gentle, especially the blond who held a gun instead of a child and shoved her every third step she took.

"He might just kill us for this. If anybody sees, we're dead. We need to get out of here, fast."

"So we don't tell him, right? He'd just get angry," the man carrying Sage answered. "She sure ain't going to tell him. Mack will never know they got loose. Besides, we got 'em back, didn't we? And we still have another twenty before we're supposed to leave and... you know."

Leave?

Yes, he'd cocked his head toward her. So what did he mean? Leave them or leave with them, taking them to a new location? Or maybe they planned to leave them here after killing them?

Once again she wished that she'd been brave or lucky enough to leave earlier, before the bars on the street had closed. Food trucks were normally one of the last things to leave the now-empty parking lot.

"You need to call 911 for your friend," Tracey told the men, trying to gauge their humanity. "He's very ill and needs emergency care"

"So he's sick. He'll get over it." Gun in hand, he shoved her through the outer door.

Would they call 911? If she admitted why he needed help they'd know for certain that she'd planned her escape instead of taking advantage of their guard being sick. Ultimately, she didn't want the weight of his death on her shoulders.

"I injected him with insulin and he's going into hypoglycemic shock." They ignored her as they entered the building they'd just escaped from. "Can't you drop him at the clinic with a note? He may die."

"That's on your head, lady. You're the one that gave it to him and he was stupid enough to let ya."

They pushed her into the toy room, Sage right behind her. The one holding the gun stuck the barrel under her chin and moved close to her face. His minty breath a stark contrast to the threats. "You listen to me, lady. Stay in line or we're getting rid of you no matter what Mack says."

Then bolted the door.

"Oh my!" She cried out before realizing she needed to control herself for the kids.

"What's wrong, Trace Trace?" Sage asked.

Jackson didn't say anything. He went to the mattress, saw it was full with the young man she'd injected and lay down next to the wall using a teddy bear for a pillow.

"When can we go home?"

"Soon, honey. Soon." She pulled the little girl into her arms and rocked her by shifting her weight from foot to foot. Her long hair was tangled again. She'd finger-comb it after breakfast.

"Did Daddy forget about us?"

"Oh no, baby. He loves you and is doing everything he can to get you back to him."

It took only a few minutes to get Sage to drift off to sleep. She adjusted the children on a blanket and used the secondhand animals to make them comfortable and feel safe.

The young guard wasn't comatose. He roused a little, making her heart a little lighter. He was clammy with sweat, so she used the water from the water bottle to dampen a couple of doll dresses and wiped his brow, trying to make him more comfortable. She would never be able to do that again knowing that the outcome might mean somebody would die.

Sitting still in the predawn hours she remembered something odd about their captors…she knew what they looked like. While chasing her, they'd left their masks behind. She could identify them. This development couldn't be good.

It was her fault for trying to escape. But she had been right about telling Josh the whiskey was in the center of the house. At least she knew they were definitely in the heart of Waco. She prayed that he'd be able to find them.

That line was getting old. Of course she'd hope for that. But she couldn't focus on it, either. She'd do her job and think of another way out of this room. Her life wasn't a series of rescues.

She'd walked away from all that when she turned twenty-one. "Heck, I even changed my name to avoid it." *Pick yourself up and get your head on straight, Tracella Sharon Cassidy Bass.* That was her grandmother's voice talking from her overly pink bedroom. Ha! Years ago Grandma Sweetie had declared that her pieces of advice would come in handy. But Tracey bet even Sweetie wouldn't have imagined this scenario.

She looked at the man in the corner. He was just a man now. Not a creep, not an abductor with a gun—just a young man who needed help. No one deserved to die. And she'd help as best she could. She turned the water bottle upside down and got the last drops onto the cloth.

After she'd cooled their guard's forehead, she decided to talk with the other two guards. She knocked on the door trying not to wake up the kids. Then she knocked a little more forcibly.

"What?" one of them shouted through the wood.

"We need more water."

"Not now."

"Even another bottle for your friend?" She tapped on the door, attempting to get an answer.

"Lady, you need to shut up so we can figure this out."

"There's water in the tan bag you took from me." They'd even taken the kids' backpacks with their toys.

"Yeah, like we're giving that back."

"You have to. It has Jackson's insulin and supplies."

"Isn't that what you stuck in Toby—I mean Mack? One of them insulin needles, right? And you said he could die. So no way. I ain't letting you have it back. Needles are dangerous, man."

There was arguing. Raised voices. Lowered voices.

"Don't matter anyway. We're supposed to head out."

"Are you…are you leaving us? Please unlock the door before—" She tripped backward as the door was pushed open. The gun took her by surprise. When it was pointed at her head, street gangster style, she could only raise her hands and say, "Don't shoot."

"We ain't shooting you, lady. But we don't trust you neither. Get the kids. We're leaving."

"Where are you taking us?"

"Does it matter?" the blond holding the gun in her face said.

"To the airport. He dead yet?" asked the other as he hurried to the corner where the kids were.

"Shut up, you idiot," the blond man insisted. "First you use Toby's name. And dammit, thanks to him," he pointed at the ill man, "she's seen our faces."

She remembered what Josh had said. The kidnappers would feel safe as long as their identities were secret. Would they kill her and the kids now that they weren't? "He, uh, still needs a doctor, but I think he'll be okay."

"That's good I guess."

"No it's not," said the blond, waving the gun like an extension of talking with his hands. "What if somebody finds him? What if he talks?"

"Do we shoot him then?"

"What? You can't— He's unarmed and helpless." Tracey would have pleaded more but the men looked at each other as if she was crazy.

Maybe she was, since they were obviously ready to shoot her and the kids. Now they were going to taking them to a new place? Or could it possibly be...

"Is this an exchange at the airport? Who told you to bring us?"

"We don't do names, lady. We just do what we're told, and then we're gone."

"So there's no reason to kill him." She pointed to the unconscious guy. "You can just leave him here."

"We don't have time, man. If you want to plug him, go ahead. My hands are full." The second man pulled a sleepy Jackson into his arms.

The blond one lifted Sage. She squirmed and pushed at his shoulders. "I want Trace Trace."

Then she began to cry. For real, not a fake cry to get her way. She was genuinely scared of the man who held her and had a gun pressed against her back.

"Here, let me take her." Tracey held out her arms and Sage threw herself backward, nearly falling between them.

The children were old enough to understand guns. Even at four and a half the twins knew about tension and that guns were dangerous. Their father was a Texas Ranger and had weapons in the house—inside a lock-box and gun cabinet—but they'd already had lectures about how they were weapons and weapons were dangerous.

Sage had watched the gun being waved around. She'd heard the discussion about shooting someone. She could tell things weren't right no matter how many toys were in the room.

"Let's get gone," the blond said. "Mack's expecting us to be there."

Tracey didn't want to draw their attention to the man in the corner, so she grabbed a toy bear for Sage to latch onto and left their backpacks. There were spare crackers and juice in the emergency kit that could tide them over until they received food.

They had almost reached the back door when she asked the blond, "The tan bag with his supplies. Where did it go?"

"Get in the van." He shoved her forward to the back stoop.

"We have to have that bag."

"You ain't jabbin' me with anything."

"No, we can't go without it. Jackson needs it."

"Should have thought 'bout that before you made Toby sick." The second guy put Jackson in her arms after she put Sage in the van.

"Where do I sit?" Sage asked, following with a huge sniff from her tears.

No seats. The panel van had nothing but a smelly old horsehair blanket.

"What an adventure, Sage. You and your new bear friend can help me hold Jackson."

She put the bear on the metal floor and Sage sat cross-legged next to it, then dropped her head onto her hands. Jackson woke up, rubbed his eyes and moved next to the bear, imitating his sister. Sage pursed her lips and Jackson mimicked or answered. Sometimes the twin language was hard to interpret.

The van door closed and they pulled out of the parking lot. It was still before dawn on Sunday morning. Too early for anyone to have noticed them being moved along by gunpoint. A lot of people went to church in Waco, but not *this* early.

Even if someone saw them sitting on the floor of the panel van, no one would think anything suspicious. All they could do was cooperate.

"Trace Trace?" Jackson nudged her leg. "I'm tired and hungry. Where are my snacks?"

"We'll have to wait for breakfast, big boy."

Jackson threw himself backward and stiffened his body. His small fist hit her bruised jaw. She clamped down on the long "ouch" that wanted to escape. It wasn't his fault and she refused to upset him more. When his blood sugar began to get low he became angry and quarrelsome. It was one of the first clues that his levels needed to be adjusted.

"Jackson's always 'posed to have crackers," Sage told her. "He's starting to get a little mean, Trace Trace."

"I know, honey, but they got left with the toys."

Sage leaned closer putting her hand close to her mouth, indicating she didn't want the men to hear her. "Is that man really going to die?"

"No, baby. His sugar's a little low right now, but he's going to be fine."

"That's good."

Tracey held tightly to the sides of the van and the kids held tightly to her. Fortunately, it wasn't a long ride to the Waco Regional Airport. This place wasn't huge by any means. She'd flown home from here several times before she'd turned twenty-one.

Maybe knowing the layout of the airport would be an advantage. If she was given a chance to run, she'd know where to go. But had the Macks hinted at an exchange. Her mind was racing in circles trying to figure it out.

After a few minutes she realized they weren't going to the airport. At least not the one in Waco. The twins fell asleep quickly enough with the rocking motion of the van.

The two men didn't speak to give her additional clues. She couldn't really see scenery out the back window, but it was mainly the black night sky and an occasional streetlamp. She tightened her arms around the kidlets, closed her eyes and concentrated solely on not being scared.

Very scared.

Chapter Fifteen

Kill Tenoreno? Mack wanted him to kill Tenoreno? The person pulling the strings didn't want their leader out of the country? Or who did they bring him here to kill? Less and less about this operation was making sense. He kept coming back to why him and why kidnap his kids? If he could determine the answer to that complicated question, then he might find the solution.

Why tell him to kill the prisoner? Why did they want Tenoreno dead? Why did they bring Josh to pull the trigger? A political nightmare for one. They'd prosecute him and persecute the Texas Rangers. He was thinking too far ahead. The problem was now.

"I'll need a weapon." He was handed a Glock. He fingered the weapon, wanting to pull it on Mack, knowing the man would never hand him a loaded gun. "I prefer my own. It's in the bag you have in the van."

In-Charge Mack shook his head. "Let me say this out loud. Kill me, kill my men, we kill your family. The men holding your kids don't care if they get a call to shoot or get a call to let them go. Understand?"

"Understood."

Thing was, Bryce would be waiting in that hangar, protecting Tenoreno. He wasn't just going to let Josh walk in and shoot anyone. Company F was prepared for an attack to hijack a plane, not massacre everyone. The Mack gang loaded and checked the machine pistols. A lot of men were about to be killed unless he did something.

Or just did what they wanted.

"Your plan doesn't make sense. You can't be certain I won't point this at the wrong person." He aimed the Glock at Mack's head. Three of the leader's men immediately pointed machine pistols at his.

"Hold on, give the Major time to accept the inevitable."

"And what would that be?"

"Mack." In-Charge pointed to the man to his right. "Dial."

Josh aimed his barrel at the night sky. "Point taken."

"You are a useful tool to get us inside the plane… for the moment. Just don't push me again."

Mack waved off the guns and took a step closer to Josh. "Between you and me, I didn't like this plan. Never liked depending on the emotional state of an anxious father. Give me solid logic."

He clapped Josh on the back, took his Glock and removed an empty magazine.

"Then you don't expect me to kill Tenoreno."

"I never depend on anyone with the exception of

myself." Mack handed him the gun, nodded to the guy with his phone out and went about his business.

Josh was just a way to get into that hangar. A way to get on that plane. Why? He was tired of asking when the answer was simple—wait and find out.

"They're a couple of minutes out, boss," Laughing Mack said.

In-Charge Mack faced Josh, having to tilt his head up to look at him. "I know what you're thinking. How many of us can you take out if you jump one of the men and take his weapon? But you still have a problem." He folded his arms and looked around him. "Which one of us is supposed to call and check on your girlfriend? Which one of us has the power to tell them to pull the trigger or let them go?"

Damn.

"Now that's all settled. This is where you pull your weight, Major." Mack motioned for his men to come closer. "How many men and where are they located?"

Josh was taller than most of them there. Ten men to be exact. Ten men armed with automatic machine pistols. It didn't matter if they were accurate or not. Just aim close to a human, most likely they'd hit part of him.

Mack waited, his attention on Josh with an expectant look on his face.

"They'll make the prisoner transfer inside the hangar. Less exposure that way. Most likely four men— two rangers, two prison guards. The guards will leave, then the plane. You made this fairly public. They'll be expecting some sort of attack. Additional men might already be waiting."

"So we go in guns blazing and take everybody out," Knife Mack declared.

"Then you don't need me." Josh took a step back toward the van, both hands in the air. He didn't know if any of the guns around him had ammo. But he did know how to use that knife. He just had to get hold of it. "Mind making that phone call before you're all slaughtered?"

"We can get the jump on those guys," one of them said.

Their voices blended together as they spoke over each other. At their backs, Josh could see headlights on the road to the airport. Tenoreno had arrived. But Josh's main focus was on the real Mack. And his focus was on Josh.

The leader lifted a hand. All the conversation stopped.

"Only one person has to fire a weapon. That means only one person needs to get close enough, but we'll take two. Along with the Major."

Tracey had described this man's eyes as frightening. Josh understood why. Black as the dark around them. A color that broke down the walls you thought protected you. Maybe that was a little melodramatic, but true.

The stare was a test. Not just of willpower. It was a test to see who would be giving the orders and who would be taking them. Josh was a leader. It was something that he'd recognized in himself years ago. A skill that mentors had helped him hone. He understood that look. He could also turn his off and allow Mack to believe he'd won.

"I've already told you that I'd do anything to protect my kids. It doesn't matter what happens to me. But what guarantees do I have that my family is going to be okay?"

"You have my word, of course."

"We both know that doesn't mean much to me."

Mack laughed, threw back his head and roared, again halting the conversation of his men. "I knew there was something I liked about you." He turned and waved the men into different directions splitting them into smaller groups that would surround the building on foot. "Put him in the van."

Knife Mack shoved Josh against the bumper. His hand landed on top of his bag, where a smoke grenade and a tracking device were hidden. He just needed to activate the tracker.

"Whoa, whoa, whoa." In-Charge Mack held up his hand. "We still need this guy. Ride up front with me, Major."

Josh was escorted up front, an empty gun tossed in his lap. Empty. The last twenty-four hours had been disturbing to say the least. Sitting here, though, was a bit surreal.

He was in a van with the man who'd kidnapped his family. About to crash through a gate and storm a facility that his friends and coworkers would be defending. When had everything gotten so turned upside down?

"Hopefully this will be really simple," Mack instructed. "We pull up. The Major talks his way to Oaks, Mack takes him out and we take the plane before anyone's the wiser."

"Oaks? Aren't you after Tenoreno?"

"Two for one. We need them both."

Knife had just given him his first piece of useful information. They wanted Oaks and thought he'd be escorting Tenoreno. It sort of made sense now.

"He might not be there, you know. Oaks. There's no guarantee." The gate flew open and their panel van continued toward the hangar. "You could have done all this on your own. You could have taken me out. You didn't need my kids." He was tired of dancing around the truth. "Nothing I do is going to keep you from killing me and…hurting my family."

"You're a sure thing, Major Parker," he said in almost a sad voice. "Smart, too. I always enjoy working with smart people. And I don't think your men are going to just shoot you. You're our element of surprise. Kind of like a flash bang grenade that cops use."

Or maybe that was the answer—he was a sure thing. A sure way to get into the hangar, find Tenoreno and run. Seconds passed in a blur as they screeched to a halt in front of the only open airplane hangar. Handguns were aimed at his chest as he stepped onto the ground.

The other two men stayed in the van with the engine running. It wouldn't be long before eight additional men would be circling the building. They had enough firepower to wipe out everyone on the perimeter before they knew what happened.

"What's the deal, Captain?" Bryce stepped from the back of the hangar. "Trying to make an entrance?"

"I wasn't driving." Josh looked around at his men from Company F. He dropped his handgun—totally worthless anyway—then raised his hands. "There's a couple of guys in this van who want Tenoreno."

"There are a lot of people who want Tenoreno. Sorry."

"They've got the place surrounded, Bryce. Whatever you were planning, it won't work."

"If they're here to hijack the plane they won't get far."

"Change of plans. They say they're here to kill Oaks. Is he on the plane with Tenoreno?" The original plan to overpower Mack's men and discover where Josh's family was being held was a bust.

"Tell the men to drop their weapons," Mack said from the darkness of the van.

"You know they won't do that, but you could lower yours," Bryce answered.

The Rangers were wearing vests. Ready for the shots Josh should have planned to fire with the weapons he had loaded with blanks. But he couldn't. They wouldn't give him his weapon. Knife Mack jumped out of the van next to him, raised his machine pistol, pointing it at Josh's head.

In-Charge Mack left the driver's seat and stood in front of the panel van. When the Rangers made a move, he stopped them by firing a burst into the ceiling. "Hold it! All of you stay where you are."

"You know I don't want to ask this, Bryce, but they've got my kids. Lower your weapons and don't get us all killed."

Bryce led the way, placing his handgun on the concrete and kicking it barely out of his reach. He squinted, questioning Josh as he sank to his knees. This was *not* the plan they'd discussed yesterday. The one that said it was better to ask forgiveness than permission. They were supposed to overpower these guys, not the other way around.

"Up against the wall, on your knees, hands on your head. Where's Oaks? I don't see him," In-Charge Mack demanded.

"Still in Waco. They were afraid he might get caught up in the moment. Maybe shoot the star witness," the pilot told him.

The first to give up his weapon and the first to give them information. Sort of unusual, but Josh didn't want to jump to the conclusion that the pilot was working with the kidnappers. You could never tell how people would react under stress.

"Get on the plane." Knife Mack shoved the pilot, then shoved Josh toward the others getting on their knees.

"Secure them, tell the others we're a go for phase two. No reason to panic. We knew this was a possibility." Mack shot beams of hatred toward the plane.

Them? Phase two?

"Join your men, Major."

"What's phase two? You have Tenoreno. Oaks didn't get in the way. You're done here. Just tell me where my kids are or call for their release."

"You are right not to trust me, Major. Looks like we'll have to hang on to them a while longer." Mack smirked.

"The perimeter is crawling with cops." Knife Mack retreated from a window.

The pilot fired up the engine.

"We'll be out of here in a minute. The others will take care of this mess."

Shotguns against machine pistols. How many would be hurt? Would he watch the men on their knees be slaughtered with a single blast? Whatever playbook Mack or Tenoreno had, it wouldn't be discovered here. His family would still be in trouble.

But maybe there was another way.

Josh's head cleared. He instantly knew what had to be done.

"Take me and let my men go. They get in that van and drive away. I give you my word I won't do anything on the plane. I could convince Oaks to meet us."

"Not a chance," Bryce argued. "Headquarters won't go for that. We're not leaving you."

"Nice play, Major." Mack was twenty feet away giving instructions to his right-hand man, then he boarded, turning once inside. "There's only one problem. As soon as I let your men go, they'll warn Oaks that we're coming. Take out the trash, men."

"This is my choice, Lieutenant." He lowered his voice for Bryce, "You know what to do once that plane is airborne. Take these guys out and warn Waco we're coming. Give the signal."

Knife Mack started toward them with crowd-control handcuffs.

"Now, Bryce. Give the order to attack."

Chapter Sixteen

The Rangers outside the hangar made their move. It might have been the last minute before the Macks reached the building, but they were prepared. Most of the gunfire was outside. Bryce rolled, taking cover farther away from the plane, shouting orders for the others. They took their hidden weapons and attacked.

Josh had extra drive that no one else in the hangar did—his need to save his kids and Tracey. His goal was to get on the plane and Knife Mack was the only person in his way.

Josh pushed the adrenaline he was feeling, channeling it to a rage he'd never experienced. All the while gauging that Knife Mack was raising the barrel of his machine pistol. "Get out of my way!"

In a well-practiced gym move—one he had never used in the field—Josh ran and jumped. Both of his booted feet slammed into the chest of his opponent. Josh was prepared to fall hard to the concrete floor, rolling when he hit, keeping his eyes on his opponent. Knife Mack shot backward.

Relentless fire bursts. Shouts. The engine starting. All the noise added to his rapid heartbeat. He heard or felt Knife Mack's "oomph," slamming hard into the wing of the plane. Still, the man got up quickly and moved toward him again.

Josh reached out, grabbed the man's arm and used his forward momentum to spin him into the fuselage. He banged his elbow hard into the man's chin. Then pounded his fist twice into the man's solar plexus attempting to knock his breath from him. He jerked the machine pistol from the man's shoulder, holding the strap across his neck.

Knife Mack didn't stop. Pushing at Josh's hands, he shoved hard enough to force Josh to stumble backward. Josh drew upon a hidden burst of energy thinking about the smiles of his children. He hit Knife Mack with all his strength. The man fell and slid into the back wall, rattling the metal shelves.

Bryce put a knee in Knife Mack's back and yanked his wrist to his shoulder blade.

Josh took in the surroundings. Three of the Macks were defending the runway for the takeoff but Rangers were flanking and about to overrun. Another couple of Mack men were face down in the dirt next to the taxiway.

Josh's only hope was pulling away from the hangar. The Cessna was a single prop engine so there weren't any blades to get in his way. He ran.

"No!" Bryce yelled behind him.

No choice. Josh was running out of time.

Time? Hell, he had seconds. The plane was turning to line up for takeoff.

One more burst of energy and Josh caught the open door. He grabbed whatever he could and pulled himself through as the plane turned revved its engines.

"Very impressive, Major."

In-Charge Mack sat sideways in the seat, holding his machine pistol six inches from Josh's nose. The kidnapper could have pulled the door shut. He could have fired the weapon, shooting Josh. Instead he'd allowed a ranger on board.

Now he extended a hand.

Josh ignored the assist and pulled himself into a seat, shutting the door while the engine roared to full life. He was still alive, on the plane and stuck with a half-ass plan for what he should do next.

Keep himself alive. Get his kids and Tracey released. That was the goal…now he needed steps to reach it. "Is the pilot one of your guys?"

"I believe his name is Bart." Tenoreno, sitting in the seat behind the pilot, raised his voice, competing with the engine. "A new employee. Unlike Vince."

Josh had never met Paul Tenoreno in person. He'd seen the file. Photos of crime scenes. Surveillance pictures Oaks had accumulated off and on for over a decade.

"Vince? Deegan?" Josh couldn't remember the list of crimes attributed to this man, just that it was long. As a criminal, it seemed Vince had avoided pictures.

It wasn't a good sign when he took off his ski mask, revealing his face. "I think I'll stick with Mack."

Tenoreno shook his chains. "Can we dispense with these?"

Mack tossed the keys across the aisle to Tenoreno's lap. The organized crime leader didn't look as intimidating in his state-issued jumpsuit. But he still behaved like a man used to having his orders followed.

The restraints were quickly unlatched, dropped and Mack transferred them to Josh.

"Gun." Tenoreno held his palm open and Mack dropped a Glock onto it after pulling it from his belt.

The keys flew back, landing against the shell of the plane and sliding to the carpeted floor. Mack left them there, staring at his employer as he transferred to the copilot's seat.

The confidence that the kidnapper had blustered was no longer apparent. His shoulders slumped. His face filled with hatred. His body language suggested he was tired, but he deliberately kept the gun barrel pointed at Tenoreno's seatback much longer than he should have.

"Change of plans, Bart," Tenoreno said, barely loud enough to be heard over the engine noise. "How much fuel did you manage?"

"I have enough to take you to the rendezvous. You didn't buy anything else. That's as far as this baby and I will take you."

"Unsatisfactory. Come up with a new location not far from Waco."

"That's not the deal," the pilot insisted.

"Your deal is whatever I say it is." Tenoreno pulled the slide to verify ammo was in place.

"What the hell are you doing? Are you seriously going to shoot him while we're in the air?" Mack shouted, sitting forward on his seat.

Tenoreno shot him a shut-up look. "Where are we landing, Bart?"

"Hearne."

"Get us there." Keeping his weapon trained on Bart, Tenoreno looked at Mack. "Call your men with the new location."

"That's taking an unnecessary risk. My men can easily bring Oaks to you later. How do you plan—"

"Do it! We'll exchange him and his kids."

Josh crushed his teeth together to keep from interjecting. He'd played right into Tenoreno's plan more than once. Mack removed a satellite phone from the bag at his feet and made the call.

"I want Oaks discredited and dead. He's supposed to be chained back there, not Parker." Tenoreno spoke to Mack who shrugged. "You've gotten sloppy, Vince. There are too many people involved. Too much has been left up to chance."

"I follow orders. It wasn't my plan that went wrong,"

"I suppose it was my idiot son, then. Why didn't kidnapping his kids work? Didn't the Rangers replace him with Oaks?" He pointed to Josh.

"That part of the plan worked fine." Mack smiled as if he'd regained the confidence he'd lost for a moment.

"Maybe they thought Oaks would kill you himself if he was on a plane with you."

"Ha." Tenoreno put the headset on and turned to the front of the plane. Mack and Josh sat silently next to each other until Mack leaned forward and added the ankle restraints, locking Josh to the plane.

"I never underestimate the power of emotion. Especially that of a father. I told my employers that, but they insisted on this ridiculous revenge plan. Wouldn't listen to me." Was he bragging that he had predicted Josh's behavior?

"Smart advice for someone dumb enough not to follow it." They could talk without either of the other men hearing. "You know this exchange this isn't going to work. Right?"

"You Rangers are so full of pride that buying you off isn't an option. Fortunately, killing you is."

"You kidnapped my kids so you could kill Oaks?"

"No, Major. We did all this to free Paul. The only way to get Oaks off his back is to kill him." Mack pointed the gun at Josh. He raised and lowered the barrel as if it had just been fired. "You see, you guys just don't stop. We can buy off other agencies, bribe or blackmail some types of guys…like Bart. But Rangers? None of that works."

"So you're telling me that if the Texas Rangers had a history of corruption, my kids would be safe at home?"

"Kind of ironic when you look at it that way." Mack leaned back in his seat, machine pistol in his lap.

There wasn't any reason to keep a close eye on Josh.

He wasn't going anywhere cuffed hand and foot. No chance to attempt anything.

"Before I waste my time trying to convince you I'm not important, tell me why you let me board. And don't say it's because you wanted to see if I could make it through the door."

"I've got to say that I admire the way you don't give up. You're here because I can use you for a hostage. Nothing more. Nothing less."

"Use me all you want. Just make the call that will let my kids go." Josh swallowed hard.

"We both saw the mess back at the airport. It won't be long before the Rangers are calling Oaks and the entire state is after us. I have some leverage with you here."

"I'm a nobody. They won't negotiate because of me."

"We'll see." Mack dropped his head back against the headrest and closed his eyes. At this point, Josh shouldn't and didn't trust anyone except himself to save his children. Except Tracey. He trusted Tracey. For one moment, it was nice to imagine what she might have been about to tell him. One moment when he hoped she knew exactly how he felt about her.

Chapter Seventeen

They pulled to a stop and Tracey felt the van settle into a parked position. She kept her eyes down, pretending to be asleep. She sneaked a peek out the windows. It looked the same as the rest of their ride. The sun was just dusting the treetops and highlighting the surrounding fields. Whatever was going to happen, it didn't seem like there was anyplace close to hide.

The two Macks looked at the phone, said things under their breath and got cautiously out of the van. Tracey rose quickly and looked out all the windows. They were at a small airport. One smaller than Waco and not large enough to have a terminal or control tower.

The van was parked a long way from any building or aircraft hangar.

"Listen to me, Sage. There might be a chance that you can run and hide without these men seeing you. If you can, you do it. Don't look back. This is important. Just run as fast as you can. Okay?"

"By myself?"

"Yes, baby." She lifted the little girl to look out the back windows. "You see those hay bales across the road?" She pointed. Sage nodded. "Can you run that far?"

"Is it important?" Sage whispered.

"Yes, baby. Very important. Somebody will find you. Promise."

"I want to go home," Jackson insisted. "I don't feel like running. I want to eat colors 'cause it'll make me run faster."

Tracey looked closely at Jackson's eyes. She hadn't monitored his blood sugar levels in several hours and had none of the necessary tools now. She had to completely rely on her experience of the last year.

Acting out, anger, lethargy, not making sense with his words—those were all sure signs that his blood sugar was dropping. She got up front as quickly as possible. Why hadn't she thought of that first? There weren't any keys in the ignition, but she locked both the doors.

"Sage, lock the back and the side doors. Quick!"

The van rocked back and forth a little when Sage moved. She made it to the side door while Tracey searched for a spare key or food. Nothing but ketchup packets and trash.

The van moved again, but this time it was from the rear door being yanked open.

"I told you she was up to something."

"It didn't matter. I had the keys to get back in." Blond Mack dangled them like candy in front of her.

Tracey huddled with the kids again, not trying to explain herself or reason with them. They were tugged from the vehicle. Tracey held Jackson on her hip and he put his head on her shoulder.

"You sure that's them, man?"

"You think there's more than one plane sitting on this out-of-the-way runway?"

"Then what are they waiting for?"

The men whispered behind her. Maybe they were using her and the kids as a shield. She didn't know. She held Jackson's forty-four pounds tight against her and wanted to pick up Sage. Instead she held tight to her hand and the little girl held the secondhand bear against her own little chest.

There was no movement from the white Cessna.

"What's going on?" she asked. "Who's in the plane? Do we have to get on board?"

Her thoughts were considering the worst-case scenario. The one where awful things happened in an isolated basement where no one could find them. The bodyguards suddenly seemed like a really good idea.

Neither of the men answered. Neither of the men moved.

"I got a creepy feeling about this, man. You get me?"

Tracey thought it was the blond guy talking, but it didn't matter. They both were armed and the only place close where she could protect the kids was back inside the van.

She'd never make it carrying Jackson, who was

more lethargic than just a few minutes ago. He needed food and she didn't know how much.

"What does the text say?"

"I don't care what it says anymore. Get back in the van."

It was definitely the blond Mack giving the orders. She could tell that they faced each other and had a phone between them. She inched Sage toward the corner of the van, ready to make a run for it. She desperately wanted her hunch about this to be right.

A hunch that told her Josh was on that plane waiting to see if she and the kids were released. But that would mean someone—like the FBI or police or Rangers—was here somewhere, waiting.

The men continued to argue behind her and she loosened her hold on Sage. She arched her eyebrows, questioning if she should run, and Tracey nodded. She looked so young and yet so much older than two days ago. Tracey didn't have to guess if she understood the danger—she did. Josh's little girl squeezed her hand, then tiptoed along the length of the back of the van and ran.

The arguing stopped. Tracey turned around, keeping her hand behind her back. Hoping the two Macks would think Sage was hiding there. She stared at the men, one arm cramping from holding Jackson, the other waving his sister to safety.

"Where's the girl?"

"She's right—"

They both took a step in Tracey's direction. Blond

Mac's hands were out to take Jackson from her. She turned but only made it a couple of steps. The van doors were still open. Blond had a hold of Jackson; the other guy pushed her inside the van, climbing in on top of her.

She couldn't see if Sage made it across the road. Based on the cursing and slamming fists against the van, then the running to get in the driver's seat, she assumed Sage was out of sight.

Thank God.

THEY HAD LANDED about five or ten minutes earlier. Mack had been surprised and Tenoreno had been rather pleased. Neither had said anything loud enough to let Josh determine what was going on. But it had something to do with meetings and putting them at greater risk.

Tenoreno was in the copilot's chair and Mack was busy sending an in-depth text. Neither paid attention to the activity at the van. The plane was far enough down the runway to make the van visible to Josh. He yanked against the chains when Tracey and the kids had been wrenched from it. He managed to cap his panic when he saw his little girl run. He didn't want to draw attention to her.

"Did your heart stop there for a minute?" Bart the pilot asked. "I know mine sure did. That's this guy's kid. Right? Man, you've got a brave little girl."

Josh nodded. He might have gotten out a yes or confirmation grunt, but he couldn't be certain. As soon as the relief hit that the men weren't following Sage and she might be safe, the anxiety had doubled as Jackson and Tracey were pushed back inside the van. Tracey hadn't run. He'd seen Jackson's form. He was practically limp in Tracey's arms. Something was wrong with his son.

"What are you talking about?" Tenoreno shouted as Sage disappeared behind a hay bale. "Tell them to go get her. Why didn't you say something when she ran?"

"Man, I didn't sign on to hurt any kids. Disengage the transponder, fly the plane, get my payoff. Sure. Hurting kids was not included and won't be."

"If we didn't need a pilot, you'd be dead now." Tenoreno turned an interesting shade of explosive red.

"We don't need the girl. We didn't need additional hostages on the plane. I tried to tell you that."

"This is not a debate. You work for me."

Tenoreno screamed his lack of control. Bart shrank a little more toward the pilot's door. Mack's body stiffened as he deliberately sank back into the leather seat. The muscle in his jaw twitched. He let the machine pistol's barrel drop in line with his boss's head. Accident or deliberate?

Josh didn't want Mack to open fire. Not when he didn't have a weapon and no control over the men still holding Tracey and Jackson.

"It doesn't matter now. Here they come. Open the door, then tell the men to bring the woman on board."

Josh couldn't see who was inside the darkened windows. Mack did as he was instructed—opened the door and called his men on the phone.

If he made it through this, someone might eventually ask him what he'd hoped to gain by allowing himself to become a hostage. Originally there'd been a lot of adrenaline involved. But it came down to being there for his kids. He couldn't let anyone else make decisions that involved their lives. And if that put his at risk.

So be it.

Chapter Eighteen

"This isn't going to work." George was compelled to voice his thoughts one last time. "There's only one reason they'd want you here, Captain Oaks. Paul Tenoreno wants to kill you."

"We have a sound plan."

"Hardly. It's our only plan. Might be a good one for Tenoreno. You get out of the car, they shoot you. Period. They have no reason to release any of the hostages."

Crouched in the backseat of a small sedan wasn't the most comfortable place George had ever held a conversation. It definitely wasn't the worst, either. At least he wasn't shoved in the trunk like last year. He shook the random thoughts from his mind and concentrated.

Aiden Oaks had parked the car next to the Cessna. His plan to accommodate the kidnappers and escaped prisoner hadn't included the FBI. George was coordinating the teams surrounding the airstrip.

Of course, the entire jumping-in-the-car-at-the-last-minute thing had caught him slightly unprepared. He was only carrying his cell phone and Glock. The ammo he had in the magazine was it. The team was communicating through a series of group texts.

"No one asked you to ride along," Aiden said.

"No, sir, you didn't. I have a lot of experience with kidnappings and abductions. Did you know that, Captain?"

"I wouldn't say you've had any experience with this kind. Those kids are still in danger because the men who outrank me wouldn't allow me to escort Tenoreno's flight. He's a vindictive son of—"

"I know why we're waiting, but what do you think they're waiting for? Is the van with Tracey and Jackson still sitting on the road? Damn, that was a brave move Tracey made, sending one of the kids to safety."

The cop who picked her up had her safely in his squad car.

"Good thing the Hearne PD picked up Sage as she ran to hide behind the hay. Sweet thing argued that she had to stay there and wait on her daddy." Aiden chuckled. "Van's been creeping up behind us at a snail's pace. Everybody seems to be in a holding pattern. Are the men in place?"

"Three more minutes, sir."

Just before they'd arrived in Hearne to rendezvous with Tenoreno, he'd kicked the rearview mirror off the windshield. It was propped on the backseat headrest so he could see the plane. The door opened but he couldn't make out anything inside.

"Van's speeding up. I'm getting out and leaving the door open for you, Agent Lanning."

"We have eyes on Parker. He's handcuffed and manacled to the seat behind the pilot. Tenoreno is in the co-pilot chair." The team kept him up-to-date with a text. "You have your handcuff key ready?"

"Got it," Oaks said as he swung his legs from the car. He left the door as a bit of protection between him and the plane.

George dialed Kendall's number, ready to get the advance started with his men. He'd pass along information, but his phone was on silent, just in case the perps got close enough to hear him. Then he angled the mirror, attempting to find any guns pointed in their direction. They knew from looking through the windows that at least two hostiles were aboard, maybe three.

The Rangers in Huntsville had stated that only the kidnapper who gave the orders was on board. Bart Temple, the pilot, already had an open investigation about his suspicious activities. The report from the airplane hangar suggested that he had supplied information and had voluntarily gotten on the plane.

"Air traffic has been diverted. We have a helicopter standing by in case we need it."

The van squealed to a stop.

"Where are you going?" a man shouted.

George turned the mirror. "One man, armed with a Glock. Nervous. Anxious. Unpredictable. No eyes on Tracey or the boy."

"Move to the door, Oaks," a voice inside the plane said.

"I ain't no rookie. Release Parker and the other hostages."

"The Major is cozy and staying where he is."

"Then so am I." Oaks sat on the seat.

George knew what the captain was doing. It didn't make it any easier to wait on the kidnappers' next move.

Tracey screamed and George could only imagine what the kidnappers had done to elicit her reaction. Damn, he hated being blind. He whipped the mirror around to see the driver pulling Tracey past the steering wheel. Soon they were joined by his partner, who carried Jackson.

"The kid looks ill. I repeat, the kid looks ill and won't be able to run on his own."

"Hey, you guys in the plane." The driver pushed the barrel of his handgun under Tracey's chin. "Or inside the car. Whoever cares about this woman! You better give us a way out of here or she and the kid are going to get it."

"Yeah," the one cradling Jackson said. "We want our own plane. Or you can kick these bastards out and we'll take this one."

"I can get another plane here. Why don't you give me the kid to show good faith?" Oaks tried to negotiate.

"Oh no. No way! We keep both of them." They argued.

The man holding Jackson started waving his handgun, then smashed it against his own forehead, proving that he was losing it. If he touched the kid, nothing would hold George inside the car.

Everyone on the team hated unpredictable kidnappers. The ones who began to panic. The ones who were sweating buckets, were probably high as a kite and who made everything about his job high risk.

"That's a shame." Oaks raised his voice to be heard over the Cessna's engine. "We have a sweet private jet not too far away. We could have it here in ten minutes."

"Call 'em!"

"Sorry, can't do that until I have a hostage."

"Man, I just want to be gone." He pushed Jackson into Tracey's arms and climbed back into the van.

"Ron, what are you— Hey! Hey!" he screamed into his phone as the door swung halfway shut. "We're getting on that plane no matter what you say!"

He placed his gun at Tracey's throat and started her moving, carrying Jackson toward the plane.

Whether it was their intention or not, they'd parked the van partially in the path of the Cessna. To reach the open door, they had to walk close to the sedan. The men now calling the shots, hidden on the east side of the buildings, sent instructions.

"Captain, if there's an opportunity to rescue Jackson, McCaffrey wants us to take it."

"Are they seeing what we're seeing?" Oaks asked in a low voice. "The kidnappers are panicking. We can't startle these guys."

George wasn't certain if McCaffrey had a good grasp on the situation or not. He could hear the chatter in the background. Hear the arguing over what the best move might be. When the best-case scenario came up, he thought they'd back up his plan.

Jackson looked unconscious and unaware that he was being carried to the plane. Tracey stumbled because the remaining captor's gun was still at her throat and pushing her chin upward. George watched behind him with the help of the mirror. Feeling as helpless as Josh Parker.

The phone buzzed on his chest with another message from his partner. McCaffrey was about to blow a gasket because he hadn't burst out of the car and done anything. George rolled to his side, hiding behind the dark-tinted windows for a better view.

The two men were met at the plane door with a machine pistol. "Send the boy up. Then the woman."

"You dirty rotten son of a bitch! You ain't leaving us here to go to jail." The man holding Tracey turned in circles, always bringing her between him and any of the men who might have a shot.

"Take me." Captain Oaks moved slowly from behind the car door with his hands in the air. "Leave the kid in the car and take me. They'll let you on the plane if you bring me."

George was ready to spring into action. "That is not the plan."

Josh looked through the open door and saw Tracey stumble. Whatever was being said outside, he couldn't hear because of the yelling in the small plane.

"Give me the gun so I can shoot him myself." Tenoreno held out his hand, expecting Mack to drop his weapon into it. The older man climbed between the front seats and stuck his hand out again.

"Buckle in, Paul. Bart, get this plane in the air."

"Oaks is standing right there, dammit." Tenoreno pointed. "Shoot him."

"So are the FBI and more Rangers. Even if you can't see them, they have to be here. Oaks isn't stupid. He wouldn't come alone."

Mack was right, but Josh wasn't going to agree with him. He kept his head down and his mouth shut, continuing his search for something he could use to free himself. Unfortunately, the plane had been checked for that sort of material before transporting a prisoner.

"I want him dead. It's the reason we're here."

"I could have taken care of this. I had men in Waco ready to do the job after they got rid of the hostages." Mack explained. "But you had to detour and involve the kids again, making everybody on edge."

"Those incompetent jerks." Tenoreno pointed to the men holding Tracey.

"Someone has confused them." Mack pointedly looked at Tenoreno. "Now they believe they've been double-crossed. Their position is kind of natural."

"Don't take that tone with me, Vince. I know where your kid lives."

Vince, Mack, whatever the hell his name was, didn't like Paul Tenoreno. His knuckles turned a bright white, fisted as they were around the machine pistol grip. The plane shifted slightly to the side as someone climbed up the steps.

The blond guy who had been holding Tracey backed onto the plane—slowly, sticking his foot out behind him while he wrapped one arm around someone's throat. Josh had to pull his legs and feet out of the way. He didn't want the man to fall and choke… Aiden.

A shot of relief hit Josh. He didn't want anyone else on the plane, but knowing Tracey wasn't gave him a little hope she and Jackson might make it out of this situation alive.

"Good to see you alive, son," Aiden said to Josh as the new guy shoved him onto the empty seat.

"Captain Oaks." Tenoreno was halfway between the seats.

"Fancy meeting you here, Paul," Aiden taunted. "You okay, kid?" he asked Josh in a lower voice.

Tenoreno's fists hit both of the seat backs. "Shut up before I shoot you dead. Your blood would be splattered against this white leather in a heartbeat if we didn't need to leave."

"You don't trust that they'll let you?" Aiden taunted.

The result was another beet-red rise in Tenoreno's color. The man definitely didn't have control of his temper. And Aiden definitely knew what buttons to push. Tenoreno slammed Aiden forward.

To Josh it seemed that Aiden sort of threw himself forward, then he knew why. He dropped a handcuff key into his hand. His eyes must have grown wide with surprise because Aiden frowned and shook his head.

Josh recovered and tried to shrink into the seat. Let Aiden have all the attention and he could free his feet and hands pretty quickly. Or at least he thought he could.

The plane dipped slightly again as someone began climbing the steps. The second man was pushing Tracey up, and in her arms she held Jackson.

Escaping was complicated before. Now it was closer to impossible. Was he willing to risk a machine gun blast through the plane with two people he loved occupying seats?

Tenoreno continued to yell. "Get us out of here!"

Bart started the engine. Josh held out his arms to catch his son as Tracey handed him through the opening, before falling to her knees on the carpet as the plane jerked forward.

"Wait! No!" the man on the bottom step fell away.

"Pull the door shut, Tommy, so we can get going," Mack ordered.

Tommy laughed at the man—his partner three minutes ago—being left behind on the runway. He reached for the rope to pull in the steps and the slam of Mack's weapon firing hit Josh's ears. Gunpowder filled his nostrils before he turned his head and caught a glimpse of Tommy falling through the door.

Mack leaned across, fired his weapon again—presumably at the man he'd left behind. Then he pulled the stairs up and secured the door.

"Damn. What now?" Bart yelled.

It seemed like Josh had constantly asked himself the same question again and again for the past forty hours…

Chapter Nineteen

Jackson had barely been noticed by anyone on the plane since they'd tossed him back to Tracey. The sudden firing of the gun had made him scream. She was certain he hadn't seen any part of the cold-blooded murder. She'd had his face buried against her shoulder. His hands had already been over his ears.

"Just stay still and keep your eyes closed," she whispered to him.

She desperately wanted to be next to Josh, or better still not on the plane at all. But they were, and they'd survived another hour.

"Get us in the air, Bart, old buddy." Mack grabbed a pair of handcuffs. He pointed to an older gentleman sitting across from Josh. "Put those on Captain Oaks. And loop the seat belt through them so you can't get up and retrieve a gun."

After he had Aiden's hands locked into place, Mack took the open seat and buckled up. They kept taxiing to the end of the runway. The plane turned around and not only was the van still there, a row of patrol cars and SUVs were side by side, cutting off half the tarmac.

"Same question, second verse," the pilot said. "What now?"

"Can't you run them over with this thing?" the man sitting up front said, like a minion who didn't really think.

After her time in the van, she realized these men were more like lost boys than criminals. Young men who got used by people like Mack. She couldn't let herself have too much sympathy. If it came down to it, she'd choose the Parkers every time.

"Let's try some diplomacy. Paul, get on the radio." Mack raised his voice to be heard over the prop engine.

She recognized his voice. That was the man who had hit her Friday. It seemed a lifetime ago, but she would never forget. He was the In-Charge Mack, the man who'd given all the orders.

Sitting practically in the tail of the plane, she had a clear view of everyone except the pilot. The fidgets of the men in restraints. The toe tapping of Aiden Oaks. The cavalier words that didn't match the tense, upright stiffness that Mack's body shouted.

And Josh. His glances kept reassuring her that it would work out. He'd come up with a plan. Then he caught her eye and sharply looked at her lap. There was only one seat belt for both her and Jackson. As inconspicuous with her movements as she could be, she buckled the seat belt around her waist.

She'd use her last ounce of strength to hold on to

Jackson if something happened with the plane. She was prepared. Tenoreno picked up the microphone to radio the FBI, who was certain to be listening.

"Tell them about our situation. We're taking off or someone's dying. Starting with Daddy Dearest." Mack pointed the gun at the back of the copilot's seat.

"What are you talking about? Is this a joke? You work for me. Or—" Realization hit Tenoreno. "Who hired you? My son will pay you double to escort me to safety."

"Your son is the one who wants you gone. As in forever, never coming back. It would have simplified everything if I could have killed you in Huntsville. Or even right now. But Xander insists on seeing it happen." He kicked the empty seat across from him. "You stupid old man. Did you really think he would forgive you for killing his mother?"

"You've got Special Agent in Charge McCaffrey." A voice boomed through the radio.

"They're threatening to kill me. You have to save me. It's your job! Don't move the vehicles! Don't clear the runway."

"Who is this? What's going on in there? Stop the engine and exit the plane."

Mack placed the barrel next to Tenoreno's temple. The man in the orange jumpsuit tried to squirm aside, but there was no place for him to go. Tracey covered Jackson's ears and eyes.

"Trace Trace, that's too tight."

"That's unacceptable. Didn't you see him shoot one

of his own men? He's not bluffing. He won't negotiate." Josh tried to shout loud enough for the agents to hear him.

"He's not going to back down," Aiden shouted at the same time.

Was Josh's fellow ranger talking about Agent Mc-Caffrey or Mack? Josh looked first at her, then in the direction of Mack. She could see the murderer's jaw tighten. The muscles visibly popped.

"If you don't do anything, then you've just killed us." Tenoreno laughed like a crazy man.

"Do you think I'm going to fall for that? If you're the one holding our people hostage, you won't get far. We have helicopters in the air waiting to follow you to any destination. We know there's not enough fuel on board to get you out of the country. Surrendering now is your only option."

"I don't think he's joking." Tenoreno sat forward looking out the windows.

Aiden seemed more uncomfortable. He'd moved his hands from above his head to closer to the top of his shoulder. "Why set up this elaborate prison break if you just wanted him dead?"

"He's about to pull the trigger." Tenoreno's voice shook into the radio.

Was Mack about to shoot? Tracey couldn't tell. One message had been crystal clear—Josh wanted her wearing the seat belt. And now it looked like they were going to take off.

"To hell with this standoff," the pilot shouted.

He pushed what she assumed was the throttle because the engine roared louder and they moved forward. Fast.

As the plane gained speed, she looked out her window and saw men with guns pointing in their direction. But in a blink they had pointed toward another target. There was gunfire—tiny pops to her ears which drowned in the airplane engine's hum.

The young man she'd dubbed as Simple Mack. The one left alive on the tarmac was firing his weapon. Not at the FBI, he was shooting at the plane. They were dangerously close to the SUVs before dramatically dashing into the air.

The bouncing up and down stopped, but the dipping didn't. Tracey loved roller coasters, but now there were no rails connecting her seat to the earth. It was several seconds before they stabilized in the air. And several more before anyone released their breaths.

Jackson was in her arms. No seat belt. If they crashed, would she be able to hold on to him? *No.* The takeoff was just a couple of bumps and she'd nearly lost the death grip around his waist. She had no more illusions about keeping Jackson safe. He was kicking and crying out and hitting her with his small fists.

"Keep that kid quiet."

"It's the diabetes." She knew that. He didn't realize what he was doing and after his blood sugar stabilized he wouldn't remember his actions. It hadn't happened often, but since it had, the family recognized the signs.

There was a lot of tension surrounding them and

a lot of noise, even though she could hear better after popping her ears. Josh and Aiden seemed to be communicating by looks. They were going to do something. She just didn't know what or when.

She quickly rose a little and switched the seat belt from around her waist to tighten around Jackson's. It was a close fit to sit on the edge of the seat next to him pressed against the side of the plane. He didn't like it at all.

"Please, kidlet. We've got to do this to keep you safe," she said next to his ear, scared to death that he'd lift the latch and not be safe at all. She worked with him to get his ears popped and relieve some of the pressure.

"What now, Mack?" Josh asked.

"Don't you mean Vince Deegan?" Aiden smiled. "Yeah, I know who you are. Jobs like this aren't normally your forte. You're more of a…bully. Aren't you?"

From her new position, she could barely see the front of the plane. She heard a jerk on Josh's chains. She could imagine that he wanted to stop Aiden from antagonizing the man holding a machine gun. She hated not knowing what was going on. It made the fright level just that much higher.

"Bart, take us to the landing strip. Somebody's waiting." Mack's attention was on the front of the plane. Maybe on the pilot or Tenoreno.

He seemed to have forgotten that she wasn't tied up or restrained—with the exception that it was a tight fit between the seats. She reached forward, touching

Josh's arm. He didn't whip around, but took a look at her slowly around the edge of the seat.

She leaned closer to him and said, "I can do something."

"No," Josh mouthed.

"Daddy! Daddy!" Jackson kicked the seat, and Tracey. "Take me home."

"It's okay, Jack. Everything's okay. I bet you're tired. Maybe try to take a nap." Josh said it loud enough for Jackson to hear. One sincere look from his father and he was leaning his head against the side of the plane.

But the outburst caught Mack's attention, causing him to look and stare at her.

Did he realize she wasn't secured? It was the first time that she hoped she appeared insignificant in someone's mind. And maybe that's how he saw her— insignificant or not a threat—because he turned his attention back to his phone.

Josh looked around the edge of his seat again. He winked. She smiled back in spite of the anxiety speeding up her heartbeat. She wasn't alone. He was there and he was not helpless.

Jackson's breathing evened out. She liked it better when he was awake. Even if the diabetes turned him into a tiny terror, she knew he was awake and not slipping into a deep sleep or diabetic coma. They didn't have long before Jackson was going to be severely ill.

At the risk of Mack noticing her lack of binding, she called out, "Where are you taking us?"

"Yeah, Vince, where are you taking us?' Tenoreno echoed.

"Not far."

"That agent said they're tracking us," the criminal said from the front, his tenor-like voice carrying to the back of the plane.

"We got rid of the transponder. You!" Mack lunged across the short distance between seats.

Tracey heard his fist hit Aiden. She heard him searching through pockets and patting him down. She could see the ranger's hands tighten on the seat belt, heard him release a moan of pain.

"How are they following us?" Tenoreno screamed.

"They don't need much but their eyes. The FBI wasn't bluffing about a helicopter." The pilot pointed to the right side of the plane. All heads looked. Tracey's view was blocked by a compartment of some sort but she could tell the pilot was telling the truth.

"If the FBI knows where we're going and can tell when we land," she said, leaning forward to be heard, "how did you plan on getting away?"

She was genuinely confused.

Mack's dark eyes, which she'd memorized the moment he'd raised his fist to hit her, went dead again. He was filled with blackness that looked so empty... so soulless. "I didn't."

"What the hell does that mean?" Tenoreno asked.

Tracey saw the concerned look on Aiden's face and knew it was mirrored on Josh's. She squeezed back in next to Jackson, dabbing some of the sweat off his forehead. There was nothing for her to give him. No juice, no water—nothing. All she could do was hope.

It wasn't long before the pilot circled an even smaller runway from where they'd left. The engines ebbed and surged as he lined up to set the plane on the ground.

"This isn't going to be pretty, people." The pilot gained everyone's attention. "Those gunshots must have hit something important and the controls aren't handling like they should. So grab something steady. It's going to be a bumpy ride."

Aiden, handcuffed to the seat belt, settled more firmly into his chair and braced a long leg on the seat across the short aisle. Josh couldn't brace himself at all, not manacled to the floor.

"Can't you unlock his feet?"

"Dammit, Mack. Let her have a seat belt."

Tracey's heart raced. Good or bad. It shouldn't matter what side you were on when a plane was about to crash. Mack didn't acknowledge them. He fingered the phone, then put it in his pocket.

There was nothing to grab. She sank between the seats and braced herself between the bulkhead and the closet. As she did, Mack noticed and didn't make a move to stop her or let her move to the open seat in front of him. Jackson was unconscious. None of the shouting woke him up. At least he wouldn't be scared out of his mind like she was.

"I love you," Josh said as the plane dipped and shot back to gain altitude. He didn't have to say anything. She'd known he loved her as soon as he'd held her hand in the bodyguards' rental car. That moment had changed everything for her.

Seconds later the plane bounced against pavement and was airborne again. She kept her eyes glued to Jackson.

It wouldn't be long. Sage was safe. At least there was that.

"Hold on tight, baby." Only Jackson could have heard her, but she said the words for Josh, too.

Chapter Twenty

Josh braced himself as best he could. Mack was finally sitting straight in his seat and not watching his every move. There hadn't been an unobserved moment to retrieve the handcuff key from where he'd hidden it— between his cheek and teeth.

Once on the ground, they'd need the weapons that should be stored in the small closet next to Tracey. He couldn't give Mack time to recover from the rough ride or realize what was happening. He had to be ready. He had to be fast.

Spitting the handcuff key into his hands, he twisted his wrists until he could reach the latch. Key inserted, turned, one hand was free. The plane's power surged, trying to gain altitude, pressing his body into the seat. He fought gravity and leaned forward to release his ankles from the manacles.

"This is it!" Bart shouted, cursing like a sailor.

Josh sat up. There was no time to grab and hold Tracey like he wanted. Then it was apparent that Bart didn't have control. The plane was on its way to the ground. Crashing.

"Hold on, Tracey. We're going to be okay. Just hold on." He could see her boots in the aisle next to him. He wanted to comfort his son. There was just no way to be heard.

Nothing was fake about what the plane was doing. There was a radical shimmy when the wheels touched down again.

Noise from every direction assaulted him. At first there were huge vibrations, bounces and slams. He thought that was bad until the plane made a sharp pull to the right, tipped, and he knew they were flipping. His neck felt like it snapped in two from the concussion of hitting the ground.

Stunned. He hung upside down, unable to see around him. Then he realized he couldn't really see his hand heading to his face, either. Stuff was floating in the air. Smoke or steam—he couldn't tell.

"Josh! Josh! You still conscious?" Aiden called.

"Yeah, I'm… I'm okay." His ears were still ringing.

Mack seemed to be unconscious next to him. His arms were hanging about his head.

"Tracey? Jackson?" No sound from either of them.

"The kid's still buckled. The girl looks like she's out cold."

Pulling his heavy arms back to his chest, Josh stretched his legs so he could push his feet against Aiden's seat.

"Hold on, Josh!" Aiden yelled. "I'm pinned in here

just as tight as a bean in a burrito. My leg's busted up and caught between these things. Can you get out the door? Or see the machine pistol?"

"Give me a sec."

Bent in half and still a bit disoriented, his mind refused to adjust and accept that the plane was upside down and not just him. He managed to unclip his seat belt. There wasn't room to fall. It was just a jolt. The windows had shattered and the space around him had shrunk.

"Tracey? Jackson? Can you hear me?" He could finally see her, boots pointed toward him, lying on the ceiling. He shook her legs as much as he dared. He couldn't get his shoulders through to the area behind him. His seat was wedged in the way.

"Josh, you need to get the gun, son."

"Yeah." He did *know* that he needed to find the weapon. Logic told him that. But his heart wanted to free Tracey and Jackson first. They were both hurt, or worse.

Mack was hanging from his waist, seat belt still in place, arms swaying with each move that Josh made. He looked around on the ceiling—no weapons.

A pounding at the front of the plane made him jerk around. He hit his head on something fixed to the floor. There was a small triangle of space left where he could see the instrument panel. He carefully got closer, trying not to cause Aiden more pain.

The pilot was strapped in but it looked like his injuries were severe. Tenoreno kicked his door and it was almost open. Josh saw the gun. The strap was caught and it hung just out of his reach near the pilot.

Tenoreno stared at him and followed the direction he was reaching. An evil grin dominated his face. He moved like he was no longer in a rush. He casually lifted the machine pistol, moved the radio cord farther from the opening, then kicked the door a final time.

It sprang open and Tenoreno escaped. Josh pushed on the seat back until beads of sweat stung his eyes. It wasn't budging.

"Josh?" Aiden spoke softly, as if he were in pain. "Try the other door, son."

Crouching, he checked Tracey, giving her a little shake. He reached up and felt a pulse at Mack's throat. Then he checked the door next to his seat. Jammed. Their side of the plane had settled mostly in the field.

His head was beginning to clear a bit. His vision along with it. He checked Aiden, who had passed out. He had lost the handcuff key in the crash, but could get Aiden free with a knife. To get to Tracey and Jackson, he'd need a crowbar or tools to release the seat back. And to get either of those things he needed out of the plane.

"Hello?" a voice from the outside called. Knocks on the outside of the plane. More voices. And light. Lots of light as the door opened.

"Are you all right?"

"I'm fine but there are injured people and a child. Have you got a knife?" Josh asked the man who was at the door on the far side of Mack. Josh's ears were ringing badly and making it difficult to hear. He was catching every other word or so and letting his mind fill in the rest of the answer.

As much as he wanted to sit and let someone else take care of things, his son needed him. Tracey needed him. He wouldn't quit.

"My daughter, Jeannie… Hand me the knife. I think we can get everyone out. Paramedics are on their way."

"Let me get inside here." The man kept the knife.

Without too many words, they worked together and released Mack. The rescuer climbed out and Josh passed Mack through the door to him.

"Make sure you use these." Josh tossed the handcuffs that had been around his wrists a few minutes earlier. "Anchor him to something so he can't get away."

"You can come out," the man helping said. "I can free them."

"Not leaving until they do. You'll need me in here." Josh began moving debris, trying to get to Jackson and Tracey.

The stranger had seen what tools they needed to release the others, retrieved them and they went to work. "Start moving the dirt from the pilot's window," the man instructed someone who had just arrived.

This time another teen jumped in with him, rocking the plane just a bit.

"Where are the rescue crews?" Josh asked.

"We're in the middle of nowhere here," the teenager answered.

"They're probably another fifteen minutes out." The man moved carefully to Aiden. "Your friend has a broken leg, let's get this wreckage off him."

"The boy first," Aiden said.

"Boy?"

"My son's in the back along with Tracey. He has diabetes. They're both unconscious."

The man didn't need more of an explanation. He went to work removing the seat blocking Tracey. It was a tight fit and Josh felt in the way until they got some of the bolts removed and the seat needed to be held in place. His shoulder kept the seat on the ceiling while they finished and moved it in front of the door.

"Tracey?"

Josh needed to be in two places at once. But he let their rescuer check Tracey while he released his son.

"How long have I been out?" Her voice was breathy and tired. "Where's Jackson?"

"He's okay." Josh looked at his watch. "It's been seven minutes since the crash."

"It might be the diabetes keeping him knocked out."

The man called to someone outside the door to come get Jackson. Josh handed him to another stranger and leaned down to get Tracey. Her eyes opened.

"I didn't find anything broken," their rescuer said. "Can you climb out of here?"

"Is it over?" she asked, looking at Josh.

"Tenoreno's out there somewhere," Aiden answered behind him. "Watch yourself."

Josh looked at the Ranger Captain. "I'll be back to help. Just let me check on Jackson."

"You stay with your boy. These guys can handle me."

Josh helped Tracey through the door. She was already at Jackson's side by the time he was halfway out.

"Do you think it's too high or too low?" Agent Barlow asked, running around the tail of the plane.

"He hasn't eaten today, but he's been getting the basal dose so that should—" She turned Jackson on his side, checked where his insulin port should be. "The cannula is still here but no tubing and no insulin pump. So now there's a chance it can be clogged. The ambulance may have one."

Tracey took the information a lot more calmly than he did. He was feeling that intense uncertainty again. But watching Tracey thoroughly check his son brought him stability and reassured him. "He's going to be okay. They've called an ambulance. They'll have what we need."

"Jackson." She shook his shoulder. "Can you hear me? Wake up, baby." Tracey pulled up one eyelid and then the other to check his response. Jackson moaned.

"His skin is clammy to the touch," Josh said, knowing that they didn't have much time. "Where's the ambulance? They can test his level and will have a glucagon shot. That should bounce him back."

"We can't wait on the ambulance. We need honey." Tracey searched the people. "Does anybody have honey in their car!" she called out. "He needs his blood sugar brought up fast."

A woman ran from the other side of the plane. "I have what you need at the house. Our grandson is diabetic. I sent someone to fetch it."

Josh had been absorbed in helping his son and hadn't noticed that there was a small group of buildings about a football field away. Sky High Skydiving was written on the side in big bold letters.

"No! Wait!" Out of breath, a teenager stumbled into Josh. All he could do was shove a bottle of honey and a blood testing kit at Josh's chest. "This will work faster."

Josh popped off the top to open a honey bottle and handed it to Tracey. She squeezed the honey onto the tip of her finger and rubbed Jackson's gums, tongue and the inside of his cheeks.

The people who had gathered around were being moved back. Agent McCaffrey's voice was in the background giving instructions to another agent.

"Don't be too low...don't be too low," Tracey chanted.

Tracey went through all the steps they'd done several times a day in the last year. When this all began Friday afternoon, he couldn't remember the date he'd been to the hospital with Jackson. He knew it had happened, but his mind had just gone blank.

The memories and feelings came rushing back like a jet taking off. His son had looked a lot like he did now. Tracey had held him in her arms. He'd had a hard time talking and staying awake.

Everything a year ago had happened so damn quick. Jackson had gone from a healthy little boy to almost dying. He was an amazing kid who bounced back and took it all in stride. Diabetes was a part of his life—their lives—and he never let it stand in his way.

The details crowded his thoughts, trying to block out everything else. Four days in the ICU while the doctors slowly, carefully brought Jackson's electrolytes, potassium and blood sugar into balance. If they did it too fast, he'd die. If they did it too slow, he'd die.

The memory recreated the raw fright of that drive to the hospital emergency. His heart was pounding faster now than it had throughout the past two days.

He'll be okay. He has to be.

"What's she doing?" an onlooker asked.

"Trying to get his blood sugar up." Kendall Barlow answered for them, then knelt next to Josh and Tracey. "I wanted you to know that Sage is safe. We took her to a hospital near Hearne. She's a brave little girl and is talking up a storm about what happened. If you're uncomfortable with that…"

"You're sure she's okay?" Josh asked.

Agent Barlow patted him on the shoulder. "No reason to worry. Rangers arrived to escort her home. Bryce Johnson said he won't be leaving her side. I'll call and have him bring her to Round Rock."

"Round Rock?"

"It's the closest hospital. Agent McCaffrey gave the order for our helicopter to evacuate you guys."

The agent stood and withdrew her weapon. "Can he be moved?"

Josh saw the weapon out of the corner of his eye. He scanned the area around them and saw Mack being loaded and handcuffed into the back of a truck. He didn't want to move Jackson until the digital reading came up, but they were about to be sitting ducks.

"What's going on?" Tracey asked from the ground. "His reading is only at forty. I'd like to see if we could get some juice. I'd hate to be in the air if he doesn't bounce back."

"We should take cover. Tenoreno escaped when we crashed. He grabbed the machine pistol before he got out of the plane."

"Does Jackson need juice or is he stable to make a twenty-minute flight to the hospital?" Kendall asked. "Or do we need to take him to the house?"

"No, we can't risk it. Not unless we can get him to drink something, get his levels a bit higher. This kit doesn't have glucagon." Tracey stood with Jackson in her arms. Josh reached for him but she shook her head. "Tenoreno is out there, isn't he? Do you think he'll try something?"

She'd lowered her voice so none of those watching or helping get Aiden and the pilot out of the plane could hear.

"Agent Barlow, I don't suppose you have an extra weapon for Josh? He's a better shot than I am."

Kendall reached down to her leg, unstrapped her backup pistol and handed it to him.

He nodded his thanks. His mind suddenly became clear, remembering something that had bothered him about their landing. "How did our pilot know where he was heading?"

"What are you saying?" Kendall turned in a defensive circle, keeping her back to Josh. "Like they meant to come here all along? This rough landing strip is a legitimate skydiving school. You sure? Why land at a field with no planes that could get fugitives to Mexico?"

"Dammit. Not Tenoreno. It's Mack who knew where he was heading. He was hired to bring Daddy to the vindictive son. Not set him free."

Josh searched the perimeter of the field again and nodded as they headed toward the buildings to the west. Tenoreno was out there—both father and son. The plane crash had been less than ten minutes ago and a man could get a long way on foot in that length of time. But Josh's gut told him that their escaped prisoner was close.

"So you think Xander Tenoreno wants his father dead?" Kendall seemed as surprised as he'd felt earlier. "And he's here waiting to kill him?"

"Is it such a far-fetched idea that the son would want revenge for his mother's murder? Or even to keep the power he's had since Paul was locked up?" He kept Tracey and his son close between him and the agent leading the way. "Maybe we should see if Mack's awake and find out."

Josh trusted Tracey's judgement about his son. He

also trusted his own again. He shook off the insecure blanket he'd draped around his shoulders for letting these events happen. Jackson stirred a little, still displaying symptoms of low sugar, but he was a strong kid. He'd make it.

And Josh was a Texas Ranger because he was good at his job. He'd seen the hatred Mack—or Vince Deegan—had for Paul Tenoreno. It was possible Xander could hate him that much, too.

Chapter Twenty-One

Agent McCaffrey nodded to them, standing guard at the plane as the volunteers continued to free the men. Tracey carried Jackson, protected by Agent Barlow and Josh. Whatever her armed escort was discussing, her only concern was getting Jackson to safety. That meant to get him stable, then on that helicopter to Round Rock.

For the middle of nowhere, there were a lot of people gathered under a shed where Agent Barlow stopped. Parachutes. They were packing parachutes for sky-diving.

Tracey could see the FBI helicopter on the opposite side of the road. Mack now sat in the back of the truck next to the helicopter. One of his hands was secured to a rail along the truck bed. The pilot was armed with a shotgun, standing guard.

"Ma'am, you mentioned you had juice?" Josh asked the woman who seemed to be the owner. "Is it in the house?"

"Yes, I've sent someone for it," said the woman

who'd arranged for the honey and testing kit. "Do you want to take him inside?"

Tracey sat on a stool, balancing Jackson on her legs. She shook her head not wanting to be out of sight of the helicopter.

"No, thanks. We'll head out as soon as Tracey says." Josh kept turning, searching for something or someone.

She could tell that he was anxious but not just for Jackson's welfare. "I can wait on the juice if you need to talk with that man, especially if they might come back and hurt the kids again."

"The FBI can take care of it."

"Looks like they're a little short-handed. Go on. You can tell the helicopter pilot we'll be ready in five minutes." She was confident it wouldn't be long before Jackson was his normal self. Looking down the hill, they were loading the injured ranger on board. "You need to make sure everything's safe. I can wait on the juice."

"I'll be right back." He kissed Jackson's forehead.

Then he brushed his lips against Tracey's and ran to catch up and interrogate Mack.

Agent Barlow was behind her getting names and asking why each person was there. Jackson kicked out and Tracey almost lost him from her lap.

"You could lay him here. If he's not allergic, this is all fresh hay." A young woman stretched a checkered cloth over a loose bunch. "None of the animals have been near it yet. I just set it out this morning."

"Thank you." Tracey moved to let Jackson stretch out.

"Is he okay?"

"I think he will be. Do you live here?" Tracey wiped Jackson's forehead, now dry and cool. Definitely better.

"Oh no, this is a skydiving school. I'm taking lessons and help out with the animals. They're so adorable."

Tracey didn't normally have bad vibes about people. And after the past two days, she didn't really trust the one she felt from this woman, who seemed to be nice. There shouldn't be anything "bad" about someone trying to help a sick little boy get more comfortable. And yet…

Tracey stood. "You know, he is better. We should probably join Josh." She bent to pick him up, but stopped with a gun barrel in her ribs.

"Wow, you caught on real quick," the woman whispered. "Now, we need to leave the kid and back out the other side of this place. Got it? And if you make a move, then somebody else is going to be hurt."

Where had she come from? No one seemed to be alerted that she was there. It was barely dawn for crying out loud. So why wasn't anyone surprised that she was leaving?

When exactly was this sick nightmare going to end?

"I'll come with you." Only to keep anyone else from getting hurt. Tracey tried to get Agent Barlow's attention. No luck.

The woman holding the gun waited for the agent to walk to the opposite side of the structure. She giggled as they walked around the corner and through another shed with long tables.

The gun continued to jab her ribs as the woman picked up her pace and forced Tracey to the far side of all the buildings. They darted from a huge oak tree to a metal shed. Then another. Then another. This side of the skydiving facility couldn't be seen from the plane crash or where she'd left Jackson.

"They're going to know something's wrong. I wouldn't leave Jackson like that. Not voluntarily."

"We don't care if they come looking for you. The more they look, the more they'll flush Paul from his hiding place," a man in his midthirties answered from behind a stack of hay.

The twentysomething woman, actually about the same age as Tracey, sidled up next to the man and lifted her lips for a kiss. And, of course, she lifted the gun and pointed it in Tracey's general direction.

"Why in the world do you think you need me to help you find your father? You are Xander Tenoreno. Right?"

It was hard to be scared. Too much had happened in the past two days—she'd barely been conscious half an hour. She'd changed or she was just plain tired. The reason was unimportant, but these two didn't really seem threatening to her.

"You know… I might have a concussion. Even though I feel totally fine." She crossed the lean-to and plopped down on a hay bale. "Or I might be quite confident that Josh won't take long to find me. But I am going to wait. Right here. You can do what you want. I'm waiting."

She was the one who sounded a little scary. Sort of delusional or exhausted. Maybe it was shock. Once she sat, she realized her entire body was shaking and her mouth had gone completely dry.

Xander Tenoreno acted like he was ignoring her, as if she wasn't important. But she'd been watching men and their body language closely for hours. And his was tense, ready to pounce if she moved the wrong direction.

"This is ridiculous," Tracey continued. "Your father is long gone. Probably stole a car and headed out while everyone else was running to the plane crash."

"You can shut up now." The chick—she'd lost the right to be referred to with respect—pulled the rather large gun up to her shoulder again. "Xander knows what he's doing."

Tracey nodded and began looking for a weapon or for something to hide behind when the shooting started.

Wow. She really did feel like help was on the way. Josh wouldn't let anything happen to her. She was more concerned about both of them being separated from Jackson. He needed juice and was barely coherent enough to swallow.

Xander took out a telescope that fit on top of a rifle. He searched the fields and turned his body in a semicircle. He paused several times but didn't do anything except remove his arm from around the woman.

"Why not just let your father go to jail for the rest of his life?" She was legitimately curious. But it also occurred to her that if he was distracted, Josh would have an easier time taking him by surprise.

"My father wasn't going to jail. He wasn't even going to stand trial." He cocked his head to the side. "He was headed to Austin to make a deal. Screw me and our business over so that he could what? Get away with murdering my mother. That's what. His deal would have put him in witness protection. I have a right to take care of this the way I see fit."

Now she was scared.

"WHERE'S TRACEY?" JOSH SAT Jackson upright and made sure he could swallow some juice. A little dribbled down his chin, but he didn't choke. He'd give him a couple of minutes and then repeat the blood test.

"I thought she followed you. I checked the west side of the house, came back and she wasn't here." Kendall placed her palm on Jackson's cheek. "His color is better. Are you ready to transport now?"

"I…" He looked at his son, looked around for Tracey, then stared at the armed pilot. "Something's wrong. She wouldn't leave him alone like this."

They asked the family members and the instructor if they'd seen anything. Their answers were no.

"Maybe you're overthinking," Kendall said.

"Call it in."

"We only have three agents here, Josh. We can't cover each of these buildings until backup arrives."

"She could be dead or miles away from here by then."

"Ma'am?" He tapped on the shoulder of the home owner. "You said your grandson has diabetes, so you're familiar with it?"

"Oh yes, I'm sorry that we didn't have everything your wife needed."

Josh didn't correct her. Moving forward was more important. "Do you mind sitting with Jackson?"

"No. I'd be glad to."

Josh walked away and caught the end of Kendall's phone conversation.

"He's not going to stay put. Tenoreno's out there, sir. I can at least find out where." She hung up and faced him. "Do people always go out on a limb for you, Josh?"

"Not sure how to answer that, but I am grateful."

"Excuse me, you asked about the woman in the plane." A teenage girl holding a dog waited for an okay to finish. "Shawna's gone, too."

"Shawna?"

"She's taking lessons and wanted to feed the animals this morning."

"Has she ever wanted to do that before?" Kendall pulled out her cell again.

"No. Today's the first time."

"Do you have a picture of Shawna and a last name?" Kendall asked.

He battled with himself over whether he should go. Jackson needed him, but so did Tracey. His son was able to swallow. It wasn't his imagination that Jackson's color was better.

"Kendall, I need you to climb out on another limb for me." Her eyebrows arched, asking what without saying a word. "Five minutes and you take Jackson to the hospital."

"But he's—"

"My gut says yes he's better, but I have to be certain. I can't choose one person I love over the other."

"Better idea. You get on the chopper and I'll do my job and track down where Tracey is. Go. Take care of your kid."

While Kendall got the information necessary for her report or an APB on the missing woman, Josh looked for an exit route. Not because he was trying to ditch the FBI agent. If he could find the best route to leave the shelter, he might be able to find Tracey.

"Can I borrow your phone?" Josh asked and the young man nodded. "That's your mom sitting with my son over there, right? Can you tell her to call this," he shook the phone side to side, "if Jackson's condition changes?" He nodded again.

The boy went to his mother, pointed at Josh. He had to try to take care of them both. He'd track down Tracey. When he was gone, Kendall would take his son to the hospital. He focused.

Where would he... There. To keep out of sight they would have headed toward a tree with a tractor parked under it. It was the only place from that side of the shelter. He ran that direction and sure enough, his line of sight to the helicopter pilot was obscured.

He zigzagged across the property using the same logic. If he couldn't see anyone behind him, they probably didn't see him. Then it wasn't a matter of where he'd come from but what was right in front of him.

Tracey.

Along with Xander Tenoreno.

Tracey didn't seem in immediate danger. He could get Kendall or McCaffrey, surround the man ultimately behind the kidnapping of his kids. He felt the emotion building. He shouldn't burst in there with no plan to rescue the woman he loved.

The lines between logic and emotion blurred as he debated which path to follow. Xander looked through a scope toward the far tree line. Josh moved close enough to hear the conversation.

"Predictable. I knew he'd head for a vehicle after walking away from the plane. A shame I wasn't ready for the crash, but that surprise caught me off guard and I missed."

"It's okay, baby."

The girl, Shawna, who had been at the shed earlier, wrapped her arms around Xander and he shrugged her off, uncovering something on a hay bale. Yeah, it was a rifle. Mack had been telling the truth about Xander wanting to kill his father.

The decision about leaving had been made. The son was scoping the dad like it was deer season. Josh didn't have good positioning, he didn't have backup and he only had a peashooter revolver.

What could go wrong?

"Step away from the rifle. Hands on your heads, then drop to your knees." Josh revealed where he was and stepped from behind an animal feeder.

"Well if it isn't Major Joshua Parker here to save the girl again." Xander fingered the rifle trigger. He was not dropping to his knees with his hands on his head.

The girl got closer to his side. She didn't bother listening to Josh, either.

"Don't be an idiot, Tenoreno. I'm not going to let you hurt anyone. Even your own father." Josh stepped closer, but not close enough to give Xander any advantage. Swinging the rifle around to point at Tracey or himself would be harder at this range.

"She has a gun," Tracey informed him as she slipped off her seat on the hay.

"And she knows how to use it." Xander shifted and the gun was in his hand. "But I know to use it better."

"Give it up. You're not getting away from here."

"Funny thing about revenge, Josh. I'd rather see my father suffer for what he did. He murdered my mother. All she wanted was to live somewhere else. Someplace where he wasn't. After forty years with him, she probably deserved it."

"So you kidnapped Jackson and Sage, and set up this entire game to get back at your daddy?" Tracey moved another step away from Tenoreno.

Josh could tell she was heading for the back side of

the lean-to. All she needed was a distraction. "All this because you have daddy issues."

"Seriously? You think I'm going to fall for a question like that?" Xander aimed the gun at Tracey. "I'll let my girlfriend keep your girlfriend occupied while I take care of my business."

"You know I can't let you pull that trigger."

"You're not on the clock now, Ranger Parker. You can let me do anything you want."

"Thing is…he doesn't want to." Tracey answered for him, her shoulders rising with every frightened breath she took. "It doesn't matter how deviant you are or who your father murdered." She pointed to Josh. "That man is a good man. He'll give his life to protect you both. You'll never understand what makes him decent."

Josh's heart swelled. No two ways about it, she loved him. His hands steadied. His feet were firm and fixed. He was ready for whatever came next. But she was wrong. He loved her and would protect her before doing anything else.

Xander ignored them and put his eye to the scope again.

"I'll say this one more time. Drop the gun, kneel and put your hands on your head." It was a small backup revolver. "I have six shots. That's three for each of you. No warnings. Center mass. I won't miss."

"Xander? Baby, what do I do?" The weight of the big gun or the nerves of the young woman caused the gun to wobble in her hands. Xander ignored her, too.

Shawna looked from Tracey leaning on the hay, to Josh pointing a gun at her. After he didn't answer or acknowledge her, she didn't look at her boyfriend. The gun dropped from her hands, she fell to her knees and began crying.

For a couple of seconds Josh thought it was over. He wanted to be back with Jackson and Sage. He wanted to talk about everything with Tracey. He wanted all this to become a memory.

Xander Tenoreno pulled the trigger. Josh squeezed his.

Shawna screamed. Tracey fell to the ground.

Josh leaped across the space separating him from Xander. Encouraged by the love he'd heard in Tracey's words and scared to death that something had just happened to her. Shawna was up and running but she was someone else's problem. Tracey needed to find the gun that had dropped from the woman's hands. The man fired and she'd hit the dirt herself, not certain what would happen.

Josh was fighting Xander. She was sure he felt like he needed to eliminate the threat. The man was crazy. He'd shot his father in front of a Texas Ranger.

Where's the gun? Where's the gun?

Tracey scooted on her hands and knees looking for the silver steel in all the dirt and pieces of hay. Her head was down and she looked up only to see Josh winning the battle.

She got knocked backward when Xander tripped

over her. Josh came in to land a powerful blow to the man's abdomen.

"Give it up." Josh watched as his opponent fell backward.

Tracey didn't need to search for the gun anymore. It was over. Xander Tenoreno didn't get up. He was done. Knocked out cold by the time Kendall and the other agent got to the lean-to.

"We heard shots."

"I'm not sure, but Paul Tenoreno might be at the other end of where that rifle is pointed."

"You okay?" Tracey asked. "Can you make it back to the house?"

Josh took a deep breath and stood up straight, wincing. "As long as you're here… I'll be fine. Let's go get our boy."

"TENORENO JUNIOR'S WOUND isn't serious. We'll ride with the emergency unit and transport him and Vince Deegan to Round Rock." Kendall joined them at the helicopter as they watched a now alert Jackson let the pilot settle a headset on his ears.

"And Tenoreno senior?" Josh asked.

"We were too late. Bullet hit the lung."

"I didn't think he'd do it."

"You aren't the murderer, Josh."

"Aiden and Jackson are set and ready. Unfortunately, the pilot didn't make it. There's room on the helicopter for one of you. Who's going?" McCaffrey asked, tapping Josh on the back of his shoulder with whatever papers he had in his hand.

It was his son. His place was beside him. Tracey didn't hesitate, she gently pushed Josh forward. "I'll find Sage and be right behind you, even if I have to steal a car to get there."

Josh stepped on board, watching her, acting as if he was about to say something.

The corners of Tracey's mouth went up and down. She couldn't keep a smile as the door began closing, separating them. She lifted her hand, then covered her mouth to hold back the tears.

"Hold it." Josh pushed the door aside and held out his hand. "She's with me."

They all moved out of his way and an agent got off, not bothering to argue. Once again he showed everyone around them that she wasn't *just* the nanny.

Chapter Twenty-Two

Bouncing back from the low blood sugar levels was a breeze for Jackson. What they hadn't realized was that his right ulna had been cracked in the plane crash. He'd been so out of it at the time that he didn't begin complaining until much later in the day.

Instead of sending them home to sleep in their own beds, the FBI put them in a hotel suite in Waco. They claimed it was easier to protect them there. And since it didn't matter where they slept, Josh agreed. They were all together. Exhausted but very much alive.

"Didn't they catch all the people involved?" she'd asked him once McCaffrey had gone.

Josh had pulled her into his arms and kissed her briefly. "They're playing it safe. Think of it this way, no cooking. No commuting back and forth to your place."

And no talking about how—or if—their relationship had changed. The suite had two bedrooms. She had to admit that room service and not making her bed had huge appeal.

Sage drew pictures that were full of Jackson's favorite things and asked for a roll of tape so she could cover the walls. There were a couple of times where she ran to the bed where Jackson was on forced rest and Tracey thought there might have been a hint of twin talk. Just long looks where they were communicating, but no words were exchanged.

They were back to their regular twin selves.

Whatever happened between Jackson and Sage, they didn't share it with her, but they did involve their dad. Josh had stepped into the hall for several phone calls she assumed were official Ranger business.

Tracey went to bed after watching Josh hold his kids close, tucked up under each arm. A beautiful sight. His look—before he'd fallen asleep—had invited her to join them, but it wasn't time. Not yet.

One day soon, they'd talk about the way they felt. Right now, they all just needed rest and assurance that nothing else would happen.

Day two of their protective custody, under a Ranger escort, Tracey took Sage home to clean up and grab art supplies. She thought Josh would want something clean to wear and headed to his bedroom when she caught Bryce coming from there.

"Oh, hi." He turned sideways in the hall so she could pass. "I was just grabbing him… He asked me to pick up—I even remembered his toothbrush."

He lifted a gym bag. She assumed it was filled with Josh's clothes and she didn't need to worry about picking anything out. But Bryce looked extremely guilty. What was up with that?

"Okay. So I'm just going to grab Sage some snacks, then we'll be ready to head back. Is anything wrong?"

"Nope. Nothing's wrong."

"I got Jackson's stuff." Sage came from their bedroom and Bryce scooped her up to carry her downstairs, making her giggle all the way down.

Everything shouted that the man was lying. She'd let Josh deal with whatever that was about. One short stop by her place and they were ready to head back to the hospital.

"Sage, honey, can you wear your headphones for a little while?"

Bryce waited for the little girl to comply, then her escort took a long breath. "That doesn't bode well for whatever you're going to ask."

"I need to know what's going on. Has something else happened? We're being guarded twenty-four-seven and you're acting very suspicious." Not to mention Josh's compliance with everything Agent McCaffrey suggested.

"Nothing that I know about. It seems that Xander Tenoreno bribed the pilot. They aren't making a big deal about that because he died."

Even with Bryce's assurances, Tracey has a feeling something was being kept from her. Everyone was acting so…different. Bryce drove into the parking lot and she saw the two men who had been her bodyguards standing at the front entrance.

"Oh, that's just great! Just when I thought everything was settling back to normal my uncle strikes again."

"You want me to get rid of them?"

"No. I can do it. Will you take Sage back to Josh?" She walked up to the guard who had at least spoken to her and stuck her palm out. "Your phone, please."

"No need for that, miss. Your uncle's inside. We're waiting for him here."

The demise of the Tenoreno family, the dramatic recovery of the twins. All of it made good television and press for the state and the Rangers. But all of it put the Bass family in the limelight, too. She'd expected a phone call from her uncle, not a visit.

She entered the lobby, expecting an entourage to be surrounding Carl. He sat in the corner alone, a cup of coffee on the table next to him. He acknowledged her, she overheard some business lingo and expected to have to wait.

"There she is. I've got to go. Call you back later." Carl dropped the phone into his pocket—totally an unusual move for him. "You look tired, darling. Getting enough rest? Do I need to secure the entire floor so you can get a decent night's sleep?"

"I'm fine. It's been pretty hectic lately. So what do you need? If it's about the reporters, my name change is public record—there's nothing I could do about them finding out our family history."

"Same Tracey." He pulled her shoulders, drawing her to his chest for a hug. "But you're all grown-up now, right?"

When he released her, she took a couple of steps back, looking at him. "What's going on?"

"I needed to see that you were okay. Completely okay. And here." Wallet now in hand, he reached inside and took out a check. "Spend it on whatever you need. Buy a new electric fence or a security system or even bodyguards for a while. No, don't argue. You've discovered there are some seriously bad people in the world. Those kids need to be protected. Oh, and I'm here because I was invited."

He wrapped her hand through the crook of his arm and escorted her to as if it was Buckingham Palace. She might actually enjoy being an adult around him, but why would he say he'd been invited? By whom?

Carl stepped aside just before they reached the door to the suite. Bryce handed her a handmade princess hat Sage had decorated that morning. "I think you're supposed to put that on."

She followed instructions and entered. The room was overflowing with friends and relatives. Everyone was wearing either a crown or a princess hat.

"My lady." Carl placed her hand on his and took two steps.

The room was silent, people practically held their breath. Asking what was going on would ruin the entire effect. Carl joined Gwen's parents, who were steadying Sage and Jackson on chairs next to Josh. Both children had towels draped around their shoulders as if they were acting out one of their stories. Sage even had the wand they'd made together months ago.

Josh formally bowed. He raised his eyebrows and carefully took her hand.

"I was hoping for a moment alone before this happened," he whispered, "but I got outvoted." Josh cleared his throat. "Before we have an audience with the Prince and Princess Parkers, you need to know that their father—"

"The king," the twins said together.

"The king, loves you with all his mind, soul and heart. So...Tracey Cassidy..." He dipped his hand in his pocket and knelt on bended knee.

"Would you marry us?" they all said together.

Josh opened his palm where a sparkly diamond solitaire was surrounded by multicolored glitter. She cupped Josh's checks and kissed him with her answer as he stood.

Everyone began clapping.

"That means yes!" the twins shouted.

Epilogue

Two weeks later

"Let me get this straight. All you have to do is wait around until you're thirty years old and you get control of your own money. That sounds like a plan. You're already set for life," Bryce told Tracey. He had one arm around the waist of his girlfriend and the other wrapped around a bucket of Bush's chicken strips.

Tracey nodded like the ten other times she'd answered the question for Josh's men. Josh thought she'd lose a gasket if she discovered Bryce was teasing a fellow silver-spooner. She needed rescuing and this time he didn't need a gun.

"Did he tell you that I had to collect that rock and get it to the room before you?" Bryce said, pointing to her ring. "So you really don't have to work—"

"She does if we want to eat." Josh jumped in and stole the chicken from his computer expert. He whisked Tracey away to a corner of the kitchen not occupied by a ranger or significant other. "Sorry."

"You said you wouldn't tell anyone."

"I didn't." He shrugged. "They are investigators, you know. They all worked on different possibilities of who had the kids even when they were told to stand down. It's just one of those things that happens at my office, Mrs. Parker."

He took a chicken tender from the box. Gone in two large bites. She laughed.

Life still hadn't settled into something resembling normalcy. Maybe it never would. Maybe normal didn't exist. But here they were—husband and wife. Had he been romantic? He couldn't wait that long. He'd asked. She'd replied, "Yes. Let's not wait."

So they hadn't.

Two weeks later, the Company was throwing them a surprise party. Tracey's uncle had flown Gwen's parents in the previous week. They all encouraged them to have the courtroom ceremony while they were visiting.

"Don't you think you should put the chicken on the table with the rest of the food?" Tracey asked, making a lunge for the box.

He plucked another tender and shoved it in his mouth. "We could feed a starving nation with what's on that table. They aren't going to miss this little bit of bird."

"Bryce will. You should have seen his face when you stole it from him."

"Ha. You should see yours now that you can't reach it."

"Oh, I don't want the chicken. I want your hands free. I'm getting kind of used to them touching me.

But if you'd rather hold deep-fried chicken, then…" She shrugged and spun out of his arms.

"Okay, okay. You've made your point." He followed Tracey to the table, where she picked up two plates and filled them with munchkin-sized portions.

"I thought Gwen's parents were taking the kids to dinner?"

"They said they'd take them for chicken and since it's here—"

"You feel kind of weird letting them leave the house?" Josh took the plates from her hands and set them on the bar. "I get it. I'll take it up and explain."

"I'll go. They're really nice and I think they'll understand."

"Yep. And you're right." He wrapped his arms around her body and pulled her to him for a kiss.

The door opened and Josh watched from a distance as Aiden Oaks entered. White hat in hand—at least the hand that wasn't holding a crutch, blue jeans ripped up to the knee, leg in a cast, badge over his heart. "May I come in?"

"Sure."

"Need a beer?"

"Here, take this chair." The men of Company F made their commander comfortable.

Aiden swung the crutch like a pro and made himself comfortable. Josh squeezed Tracey's hand and kissed her for luck. That uncertain future might be resolved in the next couple of minutes.

"Hello, Captain."

"Major." He adjusted the crutch to lean on the chair and hung his hat on top. "How are the kids, Tracey?"

"Physically they're great. We're working on the kidnapping slowly. But I think we're all getting back to normal."

Josh threaded his fingers through hers. She knew why Aiden was there. Most of the conversation had stopped. There was the lull of a baseball game in the background. They'd all been expecting a decision on his reprimand at any time. Maybe it was appropriate that they get the news tonight.

They were celebrating the start of a new life.

"A couple of decisions came down the pipe today. Xander Tenoreno's been indicted on racketeering, kidnapping and everything else the attorney general's office could come up with. An operation to free the families of men who worked for him was successful. And before you begin clapping, the thing you've all been wanting to know…" he paused while the crowd came closer. "I'm returning the reins of Company F to Major Parker."

Cries of laughter and relief echoed through the house from the men and women surrounding him. Claps on the back and congratulations should have distracted him, but all he could see was Tracey's joy.

Their relationship had begun with a tragedy, and then adversity had brought them closer. His bride had the right to ask him to walk away from the Rangers after the kidnapping. Her uncle had told them he'd make arrangements for her to access her inheritance.

Unlike what he'd told Bryce, neither of them needed to work.

Seemed like all he wanted to do was make up for the time they'd been waiting on each other to make decisions. He knew how much support he had from her. Seeing it now, all he could do was pull her to him and kiss her.

One kiss that turned into a second and a third. It might have gone further, but a couple of fake coughs started behind him.

"Do we have to stay upstairs, Daddy?" Sage crooked her finger several times, then just waved her hands for him to bend down so she could whisper in his ear. "What am I supposed to call Trace Trace now? Grandfather told me she's our stepmother. Is she going to get mean and grow warts like in all the stories?"

Josh laughed and picked up his little girl. "What do you want to call Trace Trace?" he asked, using the kids' nickname.

"Can it just be Mommy?"

His eyes locked with the woman who'd been there with him through the darkest part of his life. Her eyes brimmed with tears ready to fall. "I think she'd like that."

Tracey nodded her head, quickly whisking the tears from her cheeks before letting Sage see her. "Hey, kidlet. That sounds like a perfect name. No one's ever called me that before. You two will be the first."

Cast banging on the rails, Jackson flew down the

stairs and into her arms. "They said we needed to ask, but I knew you'd like it."

Tracey kissed both of their cheeks with lots of noise. "I don't just like it. I absolutely adore it." Her eyes locked with Josh's. "Almost as much as I love all of you."

And just like kids that subject was settled and they ran back to their grandparents on the stairs. Their grandmother declared there was enough food to feed all five companies of Rangers. He felt Tracey's sigh of relief as she relaxed within his arms. The kids went up and Gwen's mother came for their dinner.

Before they handed her the plates, she gathered them both close for a hug, then wiped away a tear. "I want you to know how happy we are for you. We had begun to wonder if Josh was ever going to ask you after what he said last Christmas."

Tracey looked confused. "What did he say?"

His mother-in-law pushed forward. "Josh told us how he felt and that he wanted to remarry. You were a blessing to our Gwen, Tracey. If she can't be here to raise her children, I know she'd be happy you will be. Welcome to our family."

Tracey looked happy as they watched his mother-in-law return upstairs. "I meant to tell you about that."

"Did you change your mind or something?"

"Obviously not. I thought I should probably ask you on a date first. I intended to on your birthday," Josh whispered.

She twisted around to face him. "Get out of town.

Really? What changed your mind? Get a little too tipsy instead?"

"I wasn't tipsy. Just lost my nerve."

"You? The man who ran and jumped into the small door of a plane with machine guns firing all around him?"

"Yeah, I know, hard to believe. But a wise man once told me never to ask a woman a certain question you didn't know the answer to. I thought I did. Only to realize the only thing for certain I knew was that I loved everything about you. But you might not necessarily feel the same."

She swatted at him as if he was totally wrong. He knew better. He'd messed up her birthday and he'd messed up the romance. He'd spend the rest of his uncertain future making it up to her.

Every day was precious. They knew it better than most. And he wouldn't take life for granted.

"Do you think those two will even notice that I've moved in?"

Josh seized the opportunity of her upturned face to kiss her again. Slowly, gaining the notice of their surprise guests and family. He came away with a smile on his face.

Happy. Satisfied that Tracey, Jackson and Sage were the normal he wanted.

Josh whispered his answer so only his wife could hear. "There will be a heck of a lot of sleepovers to explain if they don't."

* * * * *

THE MONTANA HAMILTONS *Series*
by B.J. Daniels goes on.
Turn the page for a sneak peek at INTO DUST...

CHAPTER ONE

THE CEMETERY SEEMED unusually quiet. Jack Durand
paused on the narrow walkway to glance toward the
Houston skyline. He never came to Houston without
stopping by his mother's grave. He liked to think of
his mother here in this beautiful, peaceful place. And
he always brought flowers. Today he'd brought her favorite: daisies.

He breathed in the sweet scent of freshly mown lawn
as he moved through shafts of sunlight fingering their
way down through the huge oak trees. Long shadows
fell across the path, offering a breath of cooler air. Fortunately, the summer day wasn't hot and the walk felt
good after the long drive in from the ranch.

The silent gravestones and statues gleamed in the
sun. His favorites were the angels. He liked the idea
of all the angels here watching over his mother, he
thought, as he passed the small lake ringed with trees
and followed the wide bend of Braes Bayou situated
along one side of the property. A flock of ducks took

flight, flapping wildly and sending water droplets into the air.

He'd taken the long way because he needed to relax. He knew it was silly, but he didn't want to visit his mother upset. He'd promised her on her deathbed that he would try harder to get along with his father.

Ahead, he saw movement near his mother's grave and slowed. A man wearing a dark suit stood next to the angel statue that watched over her final resting place. The man wasn't looking at the grave or the angel. Instead, he appeared to simply be waiting impatiently. As he turned...

With a start, Jack recognized his father.

He thought he had to be mistaken at first. Tom Durand had made a point of telling him he would be in Los Angeles the next few days. Had his father's plans changed? Surely he would have no reason to lie about it.

Until recently, that his father might have lied would never have occurred to him. But things had been strained between them since Jack had told him he wouldn't be taking over the family business.

It wasn't just seeing his father here when he should have been in Los Angeles. It was seeing him in this cemetery. He knew for a fact that his father hadn't been here since the funeral.

"I don't like cemeteries," he'd told his son when Jack had asked why he didn't visit his dead wife. "Anyway, what's the point? She's gone."

Jack felt close to his mother near her grave. "It's a sign of respect."

His father had shaken his head, clearly displeased with the conversation. "We all mourn in our own ways. I like to remember your mother my own way, so lay off, okay?"

So why the change of heart? Not that Jack wasn't glad to see it. He knew that his parents had loved each other. Kate Durand had been sweet and loving, the perfect match for Tom, who was a distant workaholic.

Jack was debating joining him or leaving him to have this time alone with his wife, when he saw another man approaching his father. He quickly stepped behind a monument. Jack was far enough away that he didn't recognize the man right away. But while he couldn't see the man's face clearly from this distance, he recognized the man's limp.

Jack had seen him coming out of the family import/export business office one night after hours. He'd asked his father about him and been told Ed Urdahl worked on the docks.

Now he frowned as he considered why either of the men was here. His father hadn't looked at his wife's grave even once. Instead he seemed to be in the middle of an intense conversation with Ed. The conversation ended abruptly when his father reached into his jacket pocket and pulled out a thick envelope and handed it to the man.

He watched in astonishment as Ed pulled a wad of money from the envelope and proceeded to count it.

Even from where he stood, Jack could tell that the gesture irritated his father. Tom Durand expected everyone to take what he said or did as the gospel.

Ed finished counting the money, put it back in the envelope and stuffed it into his jacket pocket. His father seemed to be giving Ed orders. Then looking around as if worried they might have been seen, Tom Durand turned and walked away toward an exit on the other side of the cemetery—the one farthest from the reception building. He didn't even give a backward glance to his wife's grave. Nor had he left any flowers for her. Clearly, his reason for being here had nothing to do with Kate Durand.

Jack was too stunned to move for a moment. What had that exchange been about? Nothing legal, he thought. A hard knot formed in his stomach. What was his father involved in?

He noticed that Ed was heading in an entirely different direction. Impulsively, he began to follow him, worrying about what his father had paid the man to do.

Ed headed for a dark green car parked in the lot near where Jack himself had parked earlier. Jack dropped the daisies, exited the cemetery yards behind him and headed to his ranch pickup. Once behind the wheel, he followed as Ed left the cemetery.

Staying a few cars back, he tailed the man, all the time trying to convince himself that there was a rational explanation for the strange meeting in the cemetery or his father giving this man so much money.

But it just didn't wash. His father hadn't been there to visit his dead wife. So what was Tom Durand up to?

Jack realized that Ed was headed for an older part of Houston that had been gentrified in recent years. A row of brownstones ran along a street shaded in trees. Small cafes and quaint shops were interspersed with the brownstones. Because it was late afternoon, the street wasn't busy.

Ed pulled over, parked and cut his engine. Jack turned into a space a few cars back, noticing that Ed still hadn't gotten out.

Had he spotted the tail? Jack waited, half expecting Ed to emerge and come stalking toward his truck. And what? Beat him up? Call his father?

So far all Ed had done from what Jack could tell was sit and watch a brownstone across the street.

Jack continued to observe the green car, wondering how long he was going to sit here waiting for something to happen. This was crazy. He had no idea what had transpired at the cemetery. While the transaction had looked suspicious, maybe his father had really been visiting his mother's grave and told Ed to meet him there so he could pay him money he owed him. But for what that required such a large amount of cash? And why in the cemetery?

Even as Jack thought it, he still didn't believe what he'd seen was innocent. He couldn't shake the feeling that his father had hired the man for some kind of job that involved whoever lived in that brownstone across the street.

He glanced at the time. Earlier, when he'd decided to stop by the cemetery, he knew he'd be cutting it close to meet his appointment back at the ranch. He prided himself on his punctuality. But if he kept sitting here, he would miss his meeting.

Jack reached for his cell phone. The least he could do was call and reschedule. But before he could key in the number, the door of the brownstone opened and a young woman with long blond hair came out.

As she started down the street in the opposite direction, Ed got out of his car. Jack watched him make a quick call on his cell phone as he began to follow the woman.

CHAPTER TWO

THE BLONDE HAD the look of a rich girl, from her long coiffed hair to her stylish short skirt and crisp white top to the pale blue sweater lazily draped over one arm. Hypnotized by the sexy swish of her skirt, Jack couldn't miss the glint of silver jewelry at her slim wrist or the name-brand bag she carried.

Jack grabbed the gun he kept in his glove box and climbed out of his truck. The blonde took a quick call on her cell phone as she walked. She quickened her steps, pocketing her phone. Was she meeting someone and running late? A date?

As she turned down another narrow street, he saw Ed on the opposite side of the street on his phone again. Telling someone…what?

He felt his anxiety rise as Ed ended his call and put away his phone as he crossed the street. Jack took off after the two. He tucked the gun into the waist of his jeans. He had no idea what was going on, but all his instincts told him the blonde, whoever she was, was in danger.

As he reached the corner, he saw that Ed was now only yards behind the woman, his limp even more pronounced. The narrow alley-like street was empty of people and businesses. The neighborhood rejuvenation hadn't reached this street yet. There was dirt and debris along the front of the vacant buildings. So where was the woman going?

Jack could hear the blonde's heels making a *tap, tap, tap* sound as she hurried along. Ed's work boots made no sound as he gained on the woman.

As Ed increased his steps, he pulled out what looked like a white cloth from a plastic bag in his pocket. Discarding the bag, he suddenly rushed down the deserted street toward the woman.

Jack raced after him. Ed had reached the woman, looping one big strong arm around her from behind and lifting her off her feet. Her blue sweater fell to the ground along with her purse as she struggled.

Ed was fighting to get the cloth over her mouth and nose. The blonde was frantically moving her head back and forth and kicking her legs and arms wildly. Some of her kicks were connecting. Ed let out several cries of pain as well as a litany of curses as she managed to knock the cloth from his hand.

After setting her feet on the ground, Ed grabbed a handful of her hair and jerked her head back. Cocking his other fist, he reared back as if to slug her.

Running up, Jack pulled the gun, and hit the man with the stock of his handgun.

Ed released his hold on the woman's hair, stumbled

and fell to his knees as she staggered back from him, clearly shaken. Her gaze met his as Jack heard a vehicle roaring toward them from another street. Unless he missed his guess, it was cohorts of Ed's.

As a van came careening around the corner, Jack cried "Come on!" to the blonde. She stood a few feet away looking too stunned and confused to move. He quickly stepped to her, grabbed her hand and, giving her only enough time to pick up her purse from the ground, pulled her down the narrow alley.

Behind them, the van came to a screeching stop. Jack looked back to see two men in the front of the vehicle. One jumped out to help Ed, who was holding the blonde's sweater to his bleeding head.

Jack tugged on her arm and she began to run with him again. They rounded a corner, then another one. He thought he heard the sound of the van's engine a block over and wanted to keep running, but he could tell she wasn't up to it. He dragged her into an inset open doorway to let her catch her breath.

They were both breathing hard. He could see that she was still scared, but the shock seemed to be wearing off. She eyed him as if having second thoughts about letting a complete stranger lead her down this dark alley.

"I'm not going to hurt you," he said. "I'm trying to protect you from those men who tried to abduct you."

She nodded, but didn't look entirely convinced. "Who are you?"

"Jack. My name is Jack Durand. I saw that man following you," he said. "I didn't think, I just ran up behind him and hit him." It was close enough to the truth. "Who are *you*?"

"Cassidy Hamilton." No Texas accent. Nor did the name ring any bells. So what had they wanted with this young woman?

"Any idea who those guys were or why they were after you?"

She looked away, swallowed, then shook her head. "Do you think they're gone?"

"I don't think so." After he'd seen that wad of money his father had given Ed, he didn't think the men would be giving up. "I suspect they are now looking for both of us." When he'd looked back earlier, he'd thought Ed or one of the other men had seen him. He'd spent enough time at his father's warehouse that most of the dockworkers knew who he was.

But why would his father want this woman abducted? It made no sense and yet it was the only logical conclusion he could draw given what he'd witnessed at the cemetery.

"Let's wait a little bit. Do you live around here?"

"I was staying with a friend."

"I don't think you should go back there. That man has been following you for several blocks."

She nodded and hugged herself, looking scared. He figured a lot of what had almost happened hadn't yet registered. Either that or what had almost happened didn't come as a complete surprise to her. Which made him even more curious why his father would want to abduct this woman.

ED URDAHL COULDN'T believe his luck. He'd picked a street that he knew wouldn't have anyone on it this time of the day. On top of that, the girl had been in her own little world. She hadn't been paying any attention to him as he'd moved up directly behind her.

The plan had been simple. Grab her, toss her into the van that would come speeding up at the perfect time and make a clean, quick getaway so no one would be the wiser.

It should have gone down without any trouble.

He'd been so intent on the woman in front of him, though, that he hadn't heard the man come up behind him until it was too late. Even if someone had intervened, Ed had been pretty sure he could handle it. He'd been a wrestler and boxer growing up. Few men were stupid enough to take him on.

The last thing he'd expected was to be smacked in the back of the head by some do-gooder. What had he been hit with anyway? Something hard and cold. A gun? The blow had knocked him senseless and the next thing he'd known he was on the sidewalk bleeding. As he'd heard the van engine roaring in his direction, he'd fought to keep from blacking out as whoever had blindsided him had gotten away with the blonde.

"What happened?" his brother Alec demanded now.

Ed leaned against the van wall in the back, his head hurting like hell. "I thought you had it all worked out."

"How the hell do I know?" He was still bleeding like a stuck pig. "Just get out of here. *Drive!*" he yelled at the driver, Nick, a dockworker he'd used before for less-than-legal jobs. "Circle the block until I can think of what to do."

Ed caught a whiff of the blonde's perfume and realized he was holding her sweater to his bleeding skull. He took another sniff of it. *Nice.* He tried to remember exactly what had transpired. It had all happened so fast. "Did you see who hit me?" he asked.

"I saw a man and a woman going down the alley," Alec said. "I thought you said she'd be alone?"

That's what he had thought. It had all been set up in a way that should have gone off like clockwork. So where had whoever hit him come from? "So neither of you got a look at the guy?"

Nick cleared his throat. "I thought at first that he was working *with* you."

"Why would you think that?" Ed demanded, his head hurting too much to put up with such stupid remarks. "The son of a bitch coldcocked me with something."

"A gun. It was a gun," Alec said. "I saw the light catch on the metal when he tucked it back into his pants."

"He was carrying a gun?" Ed sat up, his gaze going to Nick. "Is that why you thought he was part of the plan?"

"No, I didn't see the gun," Nick said. "I just assumed he was in on it because of who he was."

Ed pressed the sweet-smelling sweater to his head and tried not to erupt. "Are you going to make me guess? Or are you frigging going to tell me who was he?"

"Jack Durand."

"What?" Ed couldn't believe his ears. What were the chances that Tom Durand's son would show up on this particular street? Unless his father had sent him? That made no sense. *Why pay me if he sent his son?*

"You're sure it was Jack?"

"Swear on my mother's grave," Nick said as he drove in wider circles. "I saw him clear as a bell. He turned in the alley to look back. It was Jack, all right."

"Go back to that alley," Ed ordered. Was this Tom's backup plan in case Ed failed? Or was this all part of Tom's real plan? Either way, it appeared Jack Durand had the girl.

CASSIDY LOOKED AS if she might make a run for it at any moment. That would be a huge mistake on her part. But Jack could tell that she was now pretty sure she shouldn't be trusting him. He wasn't sure how much longer he could keep her here. She reached for her phone, but he laid a hand on her arm.

"That's the van coming back," he said quietly. At the sound of the engine growing nearer, he signaled her not to make a sound as he pulled her deeper into the darkness of the doorway recess. The van drove slowly up the alley. He'd feared they would come back. That's why he'd been hesitant to move from their hiding place.

Jack held his breath as he watched the blonde, afraid

she might do something crazy like decide to take her chances and run. He wouldn't have blamed her. For all she knew, he could have been in on the abduction and was holding her here until the men in the van came back for her.

The driver of the van braked next to the open doorway. The engine sat idling. Jack waited for the sound of a door opening. He'd put the gun into the back waistband of his jeans before he'd grabbed the blonde, thinking the gun might frighten her. As much as he wanted to pull it now, he talked himself out of it.

At least for the moment. He didn't want to get involved in any gunplay—especially with the young woman here. He'd started carrying the gun when he'd worked for his father and had to take the day's proceeds to a bank drop late at night. It was a habit he'd gotten used to even after he'd quit. Probably because of the type of people who worked with his father.

After what seemed like an interminable length of time, the van driver pulled away.

Jack let out the breath he'd been holding. "Come on. I'll see that you get someplace safe where you can call the police," he said and held out his hand.

She hesitated before she took it. They moved through the dark shadows of the alley to the next street. The sky above them had turned a deep silver in the evening light. It was still hot, little air in the tight, narrow street.

He realized that wherever Cassidy Hamilton had been headed, she hadn't planned to return until much later—thus the sweater. He wanted to question her, but now wasn't the time.

At the edge of the buildings, Jack peered down the street. He didn't see the van or Ed's green car. But he also didn't think they had gone far. Wouldn't they expect her to call the police? The area would soon be crawling with cop cars. So what would Ed do?

A few blocks from the deserted area where they'd met, they reached a more commercial section. The street was growing busier as people got off work. Restaurants began opening for the evening meal as boutiques and shops closed. Jack spotted a small bar with just enough patrons that he thought they could blend in.

"Let's go in here," he said. "I don't know about you, but I could use a drink. You should be able to make a call from here. Once I know you're safe…"

They took a table at the back away from the television over the bar. He removed his Stetson and put it on the seat next to him. When Cassidy wasn't looking, he removed the .45 from the waistband of his jeans and slid it under the hat.

"What do you want to drink?" he asked as the waitress approached.

"White wine," she said and plucked nervously at the torn corner of her blouse. Other than the torn blouse, she looked fine physically. But emotionally, he wasn't sure how much of a toll this would take on her over the long haul. That was if Ed didn't find her.

"I'll have whiskey," he said, waving the waitress off. He had no idea what he was going to do now. He told himself he just needed a jolt of alcohol. He'd been playing this by ear since seeing his father and Ed at the cemetery.

Now he debated what he was going to do with this woman given the little he knew. The last thing he wanted, though, was to get involved with the police. He was sure Ed and his men had seen him, probably recognized him. Once his father found out that it had been his son who'd saved the blonde…

The waitress put two drinks in front of them and left. He watched the blonde take a sip. She'd said her name was Cassidy Hamilton. She'd also said she didn't know why anyone would want to abduct her off the street, but he suspected that wasn't true.

"So is your old man rich or something?" he asked and took a gulp of the whiskey.

She took a sip of her wine as if stalling, her gaze lowered. He got his first really good look at her. She was a knockout. When she lifted her eyes finally, he thought he might drown in all that blue.

"I only ask because I'm trying to understand why those men were after you." She could be a famous model or even an actress. He didn't follow pop culture, hardly ever watched television and hadn't been to the movies in ages. All he knew was, at the very least, she'd grown up with money. "If you're famous or something, I apologize for not knowing."

COMING NEXT MONTH FROM

H HARLEQUIN®

INTRIGUE

Available August 23, 2016

#1659 LAYING DOWN THE LAW
Appaloosa Pass Ranch • by Delores Fossen
DEA agent Cord Granger believes his father's a serial killer, but when the attacks continue after his father is arrested, Cord has no choice but to protect Karina Southerland, the killer's new target.

#1660 DARK WHISPERS
Faces of Evil • by Debra Webb
When attorney Natalie Drummond loses pieces of her memory and starts experiencing hallucinations, no one but B&C Investigations detective Clint Hayes believes the danger she's sensing is real.

#1661 DELIVERING JUSTICE
Cattlemen Crime Club • by Barb Han
A woman with no memory turns to millionaire cowboy Tyler O'Brien for help learning who she is and why someone is after her.

#1662 SUDDEN SECOND CHANCE
Target: Timberline • by Carol Ericson
As cold case reporter Beth St. Regis conducts an investigation into her own past, the secrets she unleashes force her to turn to FBI agent Duke Harper, a man she shares an intimate history with, for protection.

#1663 HOSTAGE NEGOTIATION
Marshland Justice • by Lena Diaz
After police chief Zack Scott rescues beautiful and determined Kaylee Brighton from her kidnapper, he must rely on her to bring her abductor to justice.

#1664 SUSPICIOUS ACTIVITIES
Orion Security • by Tyler Anne Snell
Orion Security's leader, Nikki Waters, has always been in charge. But when she becomes a stalker's obsession, she'll need her newest hire, bodyguard Jackson Fields, to keep her safe.

**YOU CAN FIND MORE INFORMATION ON UPCOMING HARLEQUIN® TITLES,
FREE EXCERPTS AND MORE AT WWW.HARLEQUIN.COM.**

HICNM0816

SPECIAL EXCERPT FROM

◆ HARLEQUIN®

I N T R I G U E

*When attorney Natalie Drummond loses pieces of her
memory and starts experiencing hallucinations, no one
but B&C Investigations detective Clint Hayes believes
the danger she's sensing is real.*

*Read on for a sneak preview of
DARK WHISPERS,
the first book in* USA TODAY *bestselling author
Debra Webb's chilling new spin-off series
FACES OF EVIL.*

Natalie's car suddenly swerved. Tension snapped through
Clint. She barreled off the road and into the lot of a
supermarket, crashing broadside into a parked car.

His pulse hammering, Clint made the turn and skidded
to a stop next to her car. He jumped out and rushed to her.
Thank God no one was in the other vehicle. Natalie sat
upright behind the steering wheel. The deflated air bag
sagged in front of her. The injuries she may have sustained
from the air bag deploying ticked off in his brain.

He tried to open the door but it was locked. He banged
on the window. "Natalie! Are you all right?"

She turned and stared up at him. Her face was flushed
red, abrasions already darkening on her skin. His heart
rammed mercilessly against his sternum as she slowly hit
the unlock button. He yanked the door open and crouched
down to get a closer look at her.

"Are you hurt?" he demanded.

"I'm not sure." She took a deep breath as if she'd only just remembered to breathe. "I don't understand what happened. I was driving along and the air bag suddenly burst from the steering wheel." She reached for the wheel and then drew back, uncertain what to do with her hands. "I don't understand," she repeated.

"I'm calling for help." Clint made the call to 9-1-1 and then he called his friend Lieutenant Chet Harper. Every instinct cautioned Clint that Natalie was wrong about not being able to trust herself.

There was someone else—someone very close to her—she shouldn't trust. He intended to keep her safe until he identified that threat.

Don't miss DARK WHISPERS
by USA TODAY *bestselling author Debra Webb,*
available in September 2016 wherever
Harlequin® Intrigue books and ebooks are sold.

www.Harlequin.com

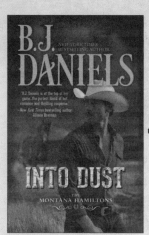

"B.J. Daniels is at the top of her game, the perfect blend of hot romance and thrilling suspense."
—New York Times bestselling author Allison Brennan

B.J. DANIELS
NEW YORK TIMES BESTSELLING AUTHOR

INTO DUST

THE MONTANA HAMILTONS

$7.99 U.S./$9.99 CAN.

EXCLUSIVE
Limited Time Offer

$1.⁰⁰ OFF

New York Times Bestselling Author

B.J. DANIELS

He's meant to protect her, but what is this cowboy keeping from her about the danger she's facing?

INTO DUST

Available July 26, 2016.
Pick up your copy today!

H
HQN™

$1.⁰⁰ OFF the purchase price of INTO DUST by B.J. Daniels.

Offer valid from July 26, 2016 to August 31, 2016.
Redeemable at participating retail outlets. Not redeemable at Barnes & Noble.
Limit one coupon per purchase. Valid in the U.S.A. and Canada only.

52613799

5 65373 00076 2 (8100)0 12169

PHCOUPBJD0816

THE WORLD IS BETTER WITH

Romance

Harlequin has everything from contemporary, passionate and heartwarming to suspenseful and inspirational stories.

Whatever your mood, we have a romance just for you!

Connect with us to find your next great read, special offers and more.

f /HarlequinBooks

🐦 @HarlequinBooks

www.HarlequinBlog.com

www.Harlequin.com/Newsletters

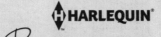

❖ HARLEQUIN®

A *Romance* FOR EVERY MOOD™

www.Harlequin.com